She looked at him, drawn by the husky sound of her name. "No, Gage. I'll admit you took me by surprise but I'm not going to go to bed with you. You're my enemy, remember?"

"That's what I want to set straight," he said carefully. "Whatever else happens between us, this side of things isn't involved. Do you understand?"

She stared at him. "I don't see how it can be separated from the rest. You only want one thing from me, Gage: my agreement to go back to Dallas so that you can do your job and collect your payment. I would be a fool to let you seduce me, wouldn't I? Business and pleasure don't mix."

STEPHANIE JAMES

readily admits that the chief influence on her writing is her "lifelong addiction to romantic daydreaming." She has spent the last nine years living and working with her engineer husband in a wide variety of places, including the Caribbean, the Southeast and the Pacific Northwest. Ms. James currently resides in California.

Dear Reader:

SILHOUETTE DESIRE is an exciting new line of contemporary romances from Silhouette Books. During the past year, many Silhouette readers have written in telling us what other types of stories they'd like to read from Silhouette, and we've kept these comments and suggestions in mind in developing SILHOUETTE DESIRE.

DESIREs feature all of the elements you like to see in a romance, plus a more sensual, provocative story. So if you want to experience all the excitement, passion and joy of falling in love, then SILHOUETTE DESIRE is for you.

I hope you enjoy this book and all the wonderful stories to come from SILHOUETTE DESIRE. I'd appreciate any thoughts you'd like to share with us on new SILHOUETTE DESIRE, and I invite you to write to us at the address below:

Karen Solem
Editor-in-Chief
Silhouette Books
P.O. Box 769
New York, N.Y. 10019

STEPHANIE JAMES
Battle Prize

Silhouette Desire

Published by Silhouette Books New York

America's Publisher of Contemporary Romance

SILHOUETTE BOOKS, a Division of Simon & Schuster, Inc.
1230 Avenue of the Americas, New York, N.Y. 10020

Copyright © 1983 by Jayne Krentz, Inc.

Distributed by Pocket Books

ISBN: 0-671-45990-2

First Silhouette Books printing November, 1983

10 9 8 7 6 5 4 3 2 1

America's Publisher of Contemporary Romance

Printed in the U.S.A.

BC91

For my agent Steve Axelrod who has more faith in me sometimes than I do in myself and who has explained to me on more than one occasion just how difficult an agent's life can be.

Battle
Prize

1

~~~~~~~~~~~~~~

She first encountered him in the chilled dawn of an English morning. Rani Cameron looked up suddenly to find his gray eyes studying her intently from the high ground on the other side of the old road from Hastings to London. It was the fourteenth of October in the year 1066, and some feminine instinct warned Rani that the day was going to be as fateful for her, personally, as it was for England.

"You haven't a chance," the man drawled in a dark voice of tempered steel as he surveyed the scene of impending battle. "Might as well surrender now."

Rani drew a steadying breath and gathered her strangely startled wits. Then she dragged her gaze back to where Harold's brave Saxon army prepared to hold the ridge against William, Duke of Normandy. For a reason she could not explain, in that moment she decided the challenge from the man with the blue-gray eyes could not go unprotested.

"I am in a strong defensive position," she pointed out softly. "My men can stand behind this line of shields and let your cavalry and your archers exhaust themselves attacking uphill."

The man nodded once, a hint of a smile lifting the edges of his rather grim mouth. "Your Saxon infantry has courage but it lacks discipline. That lack will be a decisive factor today."

Rani hesitated, knowing he spoke the truth. "If my right wing does not break formation to chase down the hill in pursuit of your retreating left wing . . ."

"Ah, but it will," the stranger declared gently. "It will hold its position admirably and send my left wing fleeing in panic across swampy ground, and then it will be unable to resist charging down the hill after the retreating men in an effort to finish them off. Across the field William will see that the entire wing of Saxons is now out in the open and exposed. He will lead his cavalry against them, and in the space of only a couple of minutes he will cut a fifth of Harold's entire force to pieces." He lifted a strong, square-shaped hand in a brief, apologetic arc. "Legend has it the unplanned maneuver worked so well that William deliberately tried it again by having his other wing fake panic and draw the defending Saxons after them in undisciplined pursuit. Again he cut them down when they broke formation and became vulnerable in the open. Discipline. It makes or breaks an army."

As Rani watched, the man reached down and moved several of the little military miniatures on the model battlefield, reconstructing the fateful Battle of Hastings, which had ultimately led to William the Conqueror's becoming King of England.

"My Saxons were probably weary," she tried tentatively. "After all, they had just beaten off an invading Norwegian army less than a month earlier, and by the time they got back to London they must have been exhausted. Then they had to turn around and march to Sussex to confront William."

"That's the thing about battle," the stranger said as he finished laying waste to the Saxon army. "There aren't any good excuses for losing. Winning is the only thing that counts."

Rani leaned back in her chair and closed the volume on the history of warfare that she had been using to set up the miniature soldiers. Across the display table she smiled ruefully at the man who had just walked into The Miniature World shop and proceeded to defeat her. "I appear to have been sitting on the wrong side of the table when you came in a few minutes ago. If I'd been working on the Norman forces, you would have been the losing commander."

"*C'est la guerre.*" He shrugged one massive shoulder and sank down onto the chair opposite her. Carefully he lifted one of the precisely molded little figures, a Saxon infantryman, and studied the fine detailing. "This is a beautifully made set of miniatures. You can even see the links in the chain mail shirts."

Rani smiled indulgently as he eyed the tiny helmet with its protective metal strip along the bridge of the nose. One large finger touched the small reproduction of the iron and wood shield with amazing sensitivity. Everything about the man was rather large, she decided. Large and bluntly carved from the wide shoulders to the muscular thighs, which had tautened the fabric of his dark slacks when he sat down. But the largeness was all sinew and bone. There was no hint of softness or fat anywhere on his solid frame. His broad chest tapered down to a lean waist and narrow hips.

Conservatively cut dark hair framed features as roughly hewn as the rest of the man. There was strength and a steady, uncompromising quality in the hard line of his nose and jaw, and the gray of his eyes had a diamond-tough gleam to it. He wasn't the least good-looking in any conventional sense, but men like this did not rely on anything as shallow as physical appearance to gain them what they sought in this world, be it a victory over a woman or an opposing battle commander. Power that was both physical and mental was a much more potent force, and this man, Rani knew, would wield it with innate skill. She put his age at around thirty-five but qualified it by telling herself that they had been thirty-five years of *experience*, not just casual, superficial living.

"Are you a collector?" she finally inquired politely.

He looked up from his study of the infantryman. "No. I have an interest in military history, but I've never gotten into the war-gaming end of it, nor have I ever made a hobby out of collecting miniatures." He glanced appraisingly around the shop. "I see the store doesn't limit itself to military enthusiasts."

Rani shook her head, smiling as she followed his gaze. "We try to cater to other interests in the miniature world as well."

"We?" he questioned at once.

She arched one brow. "The shop belongs to my sister," she explained obediently, wondering why he was so interested. "I'm giving her a hand with it today." There was no reason to go into all the details, Rani thought, mildly annoyed at having to explain to this stranger. It was no business of his that she intended to buy the shop from her sister after Donna married Lou Selby and moved away from Albuquerque, New Mexico, for the wilds of Denver, Colorado.

"Your sister." He nodded, as if having answered some internal question that had been nagging him. "Then you must be Rani Cameron."

Rani stared at him, slightly disconcerted at being recognized by a complete stranger. "I am."

"I'm Gage Fletcher."

Rani's brow inched higher. "I'm afraid the name means nothing to me."

"It will." Gage set down the figure he had been holding and leaned back in his chair. His mouth crooked wryly. "Aaron Prescott sent me."

She blinked at the mention of her ex-boss, but that was

the only outward sign of reaction that Rani allowed herself. Inwardly, however, the first faint flicker of alarm tantalized her nerve endings. Prescott had sent someone after her? That didn't make any sense at all. "Then I'll just have to send you right back to him, won't I?"

"Not empty-handed, I'm afraid, Miss Cameron," Gage Fletcher said with quiet emphasis.

"What is it you wish to take back with you, Mr. Fletcher?"

"You."

Rani eyed him narrowly, trying to fathom the meaning behind his words. "You want to run that by me once more, Mr. Fletcher? A little more slowly this time, if you don't mind. I seem to have missed something the first time around."

"It's a long story, Miss Cameron. Perhaps you would like to hear the whole of it over lunch. It's almost twelve-thirty," he added, flicking a glance at the stainless steel quartz watch on his left wrist. Steel, Rani thought idly. The color of polished armor.

"No, I don't think I would, thank you." Coolly, Rani got to her feet, dismissal written in every line of her slender figure. Her tawny-colored eyes were gilded almost gold with the force of her determination. "I have no interest in Aaron Prescott, and since I am no longer in his employ, he can have no further interest in me. If you'll excuse me, I have work to do."

Only his head turned slightly to follow her progress across the room. Otherwise, Gage Fletcher didn't move from the chair in front of the battlefield. It was going to be awkward ignoring him since they were, at present, the only two people in the shop. Rani hid a rueful grimace and went to work on the pantry of a Victorian-style dollhouse that she was setting up for display. Donna would be back soon, and if this oversized male was still in the vicinity, Rani decided she would leave. Unless he chose to pursue her through the streets of Albuquerque, there wouldn't be much he could do.

"Prescott told me you were a temperamental little prima donna who didn't have sense enough to appreciate when you were well off," Gage noted dryly from across the room.

Rani prodded a tiny platter full of almost infinitesimal fruit into position on a small shelf. "Did he also tell you I was an oversensitive female totally lacking in a sense of humor?" she asked half-curiously, her head bent over her task. She was crouched in front of the intricately designed little house.

"I think there were words to that effect, yes."

"Knowing exactly what he thinks of me must make you wonder why he would want to see me again," she murmured.

"Oh, I'm well aware of why he wants you back in Dallas, Miss Cameron." The deep, tempered voice was heavy with hidden knowledge.

"You're one up on me, then," she admitted almost cheerfully. "I can't even begin to imagine why Prescott would want me anywhere near him again."

"Have lunch with me and I'll explain in detail."

Rani sat back on her heels and glanced at him over her shoulder. The dollhouse on the low bench in front of her waited unfinished as she examined Gage Fletcher more closely. What did Aaron Prescott think he was doing, sending a man like this to fetch her back to Dallas? In spite of her resolve Rani found curiosity beginning to grow quickly.

"Did Prescott tell you I was his runaway mistress or something?" she inquired very blandly. Behind her lashes the gold in her gaze gleamed with amusement.

"Are you?" he countered silkily, eyes running interestedly over her crouched figure.

"No, but I can't imagine any other reason he could have given you for making you think he wants me back. We didn't part as friends!"

"I know why he wants you back. The reasons he gave

me have nothing to do with any personal relationship the two of you may have."

Rani flashed him a sudden, mischievous grin. "Is that a polite way of saying I really don't look like some man's exotic runaway mistress?"

Dressed in snug jeans and a plaid, western-style shirt, Rani was forced to admit the truth in her own words. Her bronzed brown hair was tucked into a loose knot at the back of her head from which several tendrils had already escaped. Her figure was slender and lacked any hint of the overblown voluptuousness one associates with exotic mistresses of important men. Instead, her small breasts gave way to a narrow waist and gently curved hips.

No, the look wasn't exotic, but at thirty-two she was attractive in a fresh, open way that suited and reflected her southwestern life-style. Her tawny eyes were filled with the promise of intelligence and humor, and her well-shaped mouth smiled easily, although there was a suggestion of stubbornness about her gently upturned nose and the firm line of her rounded chin. She could have passed as a rancher's daughter with her breezy, slightly windblown looks and easy charm.

The truth was, however, that although she had been born in New Mexico and had lived all of her life in the Southwest, Rani had never left its cities for more than a day or two at a time. A rancher's daughter she was not. The tight-fitting jeans she wore carried a designer's label, and the western shirt had been created as part of a New York couturier's spring collection. She loved the look and the style of the Southwest, and it suited her perfectly. Which probably explained why men such as Kingston Tanner, whom she was currently dating, sometimes made the mistake of thinking she not only looked like a rancher's daughter but would also make a charming rancher's wife.

In actual fact, Rani had no interest in being any man's wife. That realization had slowly crystalized in her mind

during the past couple of years, and with the perversity of
human nature, men now seemed more intrigued by her
than ever. Rani didn't mind. She liked men. In their
proper place.

Even as that last thought went through her mind, Rani
realized that her visitor was still considering her question.
She tossed him a mocking glare. "Look, if you have to
dwell on the issue this long, it can only mean you're
trying to find a way not to insult me. Don't worry about it.
I don't particularly want to be told I could be mistaken for
one of Prescott's fluff-headed women!" She turned back
to the dollhouse, peering intently into the front parlor.

"I wasn't thinking you looked like one of Prescott's
women," Gage Fletcher finally declared slowly. "Primarily, I suppose, because the few I've had the occasion to
meet didn't seem inclined to run in the first place. He
appears to be quite generous toward his female friends."

Rani lifted one shoulder indifferently. "I wouldn't
know. I only worked for the man; I didn't sleep with
him." She was studying the parlor as she said the words
and therefore missed the cool assessment of Gage's
expression, but she did hear the barely masked impatience in his next words.

"I'd rather not finish this conversation here, where
someone might walk in at any moment. Would you
please make arrangements to go to lunch with me?"

"No."

"Miss Cameron, I was told you were headstrong and
impertinent, but I was also given to understand that you
had a good head for business. I assure you that what I
have to say concerns business."

"Prescott business?" She still wasn't looking at him,
but her curiosity was mounting. What the devil could
Aaron want with her?

"Yes."

"Prescott business no longer concerns me, Mr. Fletcher. Thank God."

"Believe me, this does!" he told her with soft certainty.

"Give me a hint," she challenged, flicking a quick glance at him.

"Over lunch I will give you the full details," he promised with a shuttered look that she couldn't translate for the life of her.

Rani knew her interest was piqued. She had no intention of doing Aaron Prescott any favors, nor did she intend to go back to Dallas with this unusual man, but she was definitely intrigued now about the reasons behind Gage Fletcher's appearance in The Miniature World. "He really sent you all this way just to track me down?" she asked with a wondering frown.

"I live in Albuquerque," Gage informed her with a trace of a smile. "I expect it was more a matter of convenience than anything else that made him choose me for the job. Would you rather he had come after you himself?"

"Well, I suppose it would have been more satisfying to throw him out of the shop than it is telling you I don't want to have lunch," Rani sighed.

"Thanks!" She could have sworn he looked momentarily annoyed, but the expression disappeared quickly, to be replaced by what seemed to be Gage Fletcher's normal, politely closed look. "Since you can't possibly have anything against me personally, why not agree to hear me out? It will be worth your while, Miss Cameron. I have been authorized to make it worth your while," he concluded deliberately.

"Worth my while? This is beginning to sound interesting," Rani chuckled. "Where do you fit into all this, Mr. Fletcher?"

"Call me Gage. I have a feeling we're going to get to know one another rather well before this day is over."

"You didn't answer my question, Gage."

"I will. Over lunch."

Rani hesitated, brows drawn together in a considering, debating frown as she rose to her feet and leaned back against a glass counter full of dollhouse furniture. Folding her arms across her breasts, she studied the large man in the chair and tried to put two and two together in a reasonable fashion. No answers were forthcoming. None of this was making any real sense, and not knowing what was happening behind the scenes was unexpectedly irritating. "Do you really live here in Albuquerque?" she finally demanded.

"I'm in the phone book," he told her politely. "Take a look." His glance warmed with a gleam of humor. "I'm even in the Yellow Pages. Under 'Security Systems Consultants.'"

"Security!" Rani straightened away from the counter and hurried behind it, searching for the phone book. "What in the world is Aaron doing sending someone like you after me?" She had the book open and was flipping madly through the Yellow Pages. There it was. A small, discreet ad listing Gage Fletcher as a consultant in the field of security, specializing in business security analysis and planning. "My God!" Rani breathed, suddenly a little stricken. "Aaron's not accusing me of theft or anything, is he? If so, I swear I'll get a lawyer and I'll sue!"

"He's not accusing you of anything as flagrant as outright theft. Not yet, at any rate," Gage soothed coolly.

"What the hell does that mean? *Not yet?*" she yelped, infuriated. Slamming the phone book closed, Rani planted her hands on her hips and glared at the stranger. "I haven't stolen anything from Prescott Services, and Aaron damn well knows that! What exactly has he accused me of, Gage? I insist on knowing what's going on here!"

"I'll tell you everything," he repeated calmly, his eyes never wavering from her furious gaze. "Over lunch."

"You have no right to sit there and bait me like this! If you don't tell me what's behind all this at once, I'll . . ." Rani broke off as the bell over the shop door chimed and a very pretty woman of about thirty-five walked into the tense room. Donna Cameron had the same tawny-brown eyes as her sister, and her hair was a similar shade, but few people would have guessed that the two were related. Donna had the elusive touch of glamour that Rani lacked. Donna looked the part of sophisticated city woman from her chic, short haircut down to her expensive Italian leather sandals. The cool, collarless white pique jacket and striped culottes were perfect for New Mexican spring weather. No one would ever have made the mistake of assuming Donna had grown up on an outlying ranch, however. A more likely guess was that she was a transplant from Los Angeles. But that assumption would have been just as wrong as the one that placed Rani as a rancher's daughter. The two had grown up together in Albuquerque.

"Hi, Rani, what's up?" Donna demanded cheerfully, glancing speculatively at the massive male seated near the battle table.

Rani took a firm hold on her flaring anger. "This is Gage Fletcher, Donna. He's here on behalf of Aaron Prescott, if you can believe that!"

"How do you do, Mr. Fletcher?" Donna smiled graciously as he rose to politely shake her hand. "You're a friend of my sister's?"

"Not yet, but I have hopes," Gage told her with a slow grin.

"Well, good, it's about time she stopped going out with that cowboy!"

"Donna!" Rani exclaimed, shocked at her sister's words. "Gage is here on business. Or so he says. And I'll thank you not to make rude remarks about King."

"King?" The query was from Gage, who regarded Rani with a tilted brow. "That sounds like a dog's name. A rather famous dog, as I recall. Anyone I know?"

"Oh, for God's sake, shut up! Both of you," Rani amended menacingly as her sister began to laugh. She loved her sister dearly, but there were times . . . !

"I'm sorry, Rani," Donna managed with a note of genuine apology, although her eyes still sparkled with laughter. "I can't help it. Wouldn't Kingston Tanner have a fit if he thought someone had mistaken his name for that of a dog?"

"Donna, this is not funny! This man is here to accuse me of theft or something!"

"What?" Donna swung back to face Gage, who shook his head wryly.

"Not quite. Your sister has jumped to conclusions."

"Then you will kindly straighten out my misconceptions!" Rani hissed.

"Gladly. Over lunch." To Rani's astonishment he turned and started for the door.

"Wait just a damn minute, Gage Fletcher!" she stormed behind him. "You're not going anywhere until this is straightened out!"

"Yes, I am. I'm going to lunch," he said gently, pausing in the doorway with one large hand on the jamb as he glanced back. "I'm hungry, even if you aren't."

"What the hell do you think you're doing? You can't walk in here and make accusations like that, then just turn around and walk out!"

"I've invited you to come with me," he reminded her. "But one way or another, I'm going to eat lunch. I make it a habit not to miss meals," he added by way of explanation.

"Rani," Donna put in swiftly, "perhaps you'd better hear what he has to say." She looked concerned but not unduly upset.

"If he has anything important to say, he can stand here and tell me face-to-face!" Rani cast a glance of pure withering scorn at the man in the doorway. "What's the matter? Afraid to tell me here, where there might be witnesses to any accusations you might make?"

"Maybe." The door closed softly behind him as Gage stepped out onto the sidewalk.

"Why, that coward!" Rani blazed, coming around from behind the counter. "Who the hell does he think he is?"

"A man with a message, apparently," Donna observed

thoughtfully, eyeing her sister's tense figure with concealed amusement. "A message you're not going to get unless you have lunch with him."

"He's not going to get away with this. I'll have his hide and then I'll have Aaron Prescott's!" Rani raced for the door, flinging it open. She hit the sidewalk in time to see Gage Fletcher easing his length into a black Jaguar that was parked at the curb. She leaped for the passenger door and had it open before Gage had gotten himself completely into the front seat.

"Change your mind?" he inquired politely as she dropped into the leather seat beside him.

"You're not going to get away with this, Gage Fletcher," she vowed between set teeth. "I want to hear exactly what that fool Prescott thinks he's doing, sending you after me with mysterious messages and threats."

"I don't recall making any threats," Gage protested mildly as he switched on the ignition and checked the side mirror before pulling out into traffic.

"I think you probably would have if Donna hadn't walked in at the right moment. But you didn't want to risk anyone else witnessing them, did you?" she charged tightly. "You were going to sneak off without saying anything too incriminating!"

"Discipline," he said half under his breath.

"What's that supposed to mean?"

"I told you earlier, Rani. In a battle, discipline or the lack of it can make all the difference. I just used William the Conqueror's famous bit of strategy and you fell for it, just as the entire left wing of the Saxon army fell for it. No discipline. Just a lot of glorious, brave, headstrong impetuousness. Makes for colorful warfare, but it's not likely to put you on the winning side."

"You mean you faked your, er, retreat?" she gasped in dawning outrage and chagrin. "You weren't really going to run off without telling me exactly why you came in the first place?"

"I decided it would be easiest to draw you out from

behind your defenses," Gage allowed, the edge of his mouth curving upward as he kept his attention on the traffic around him. "You couldn't resist chasing after me and now you're out in the open, trapped behind my lines. Where would you like to eat?"

She stared at his profile, torn between incredulous anger and a somewhat shocked appreciation of how easily she had been maneuvered. "Someplace where I can get a drink," she stated ruefully.

He took her to a restaurant featuring Mexican food and bought her a huge, frosty margarita. Rani munched tortilla chips and sipped at her drink in silence for several minutes, trying to make up her mind about how to handle Gage Fletcher. He let her dwell on her own churning thoughts while he selected platters of tamales and tacos for both of them. When the waiter had disappeared with the order, Gage finally confronted his brooding lunch guest. Her gilded gaze flared behind a fringe of bronzed lashes.

"Okay, Gage, let's have it. I've done what you insisted upon. I'm having lunch with you. Now tell me the whole truth about this stupid situation. What does Aaron think he's doing, anyway?"

"He wants you back in Dallas, Rani." Gage picked up the glass of burgundy he'd ordered for himself and took a meditative sip. Across the rim of the glass he met her accusing glance.

"Tough."

"Succinct, but not really a suitable answer, I'm afraid," he told her gently.

"Tough," she said again, beginning to feel a little better.

"Is your vocabulary always so limited?"

"As a prisoner of war I'm only obliged to give you my name, rank and serial number." Rani smiled serenely and took another swallow of margarita.

"Did you really quit or were you fired?" Gage asked grimly. "If you talked like this to Prescott very often, I can see why he might have lost his temper at some point and kicked you out."

"Oh, I quit, all right. Finally. Should have done it a year ago but I hung on, thinking things might work out."

"Things between the two of you?" he probed remorselessly.

"Certainly not! How many times do I have to tell you? I wasn't Prescott's mistress and I had no aspirations to achieve that status! What I hoped might work out was the little matter of my future career at Prescott Services, Incorporated. But I finally realized a couple of months ago that there wasn't much hope."

"Because you wouldn't sleep with the boss?"

Rani shook her head half humorously. "That had nothing to do with it. It wouldn't have made any difference one way or the other, even if I'd been interested. Prescott Services, I finally decided, is, has been and will continue to be a family operation. Only family members are going to make it into the top slots. There was no sense in my sticking around, wasting time trying for an advancement that was never going to come. So I handed in my resignation. Once I'd made myself see that there was no hope of getting to the top, I rapidly decided it wasn't worth tolerating any more of Prescott's antiquated male chauvinism."

"Tell me about that part," Gage invited with a small smile.

"Why?" she asked in some surprise.

"I'm curious," he admitted.

"It's the kind of thing that's hard to explain to a man," Rani said musingly. "When you do try, you get accusations of being oversensitive and lacking in a sense of humor. All those things Prescott said about me, remember?"

"I remember. Try me."

Rani cocked her head, wondering if he could be made to see her side of the issue, and then sat back in her chair with a shake of her head. "No, you wouldn't understand

and I don't feel like being told I'm oversensitive, et cetera, et cetera."

"Now you're making assumptions about me just because I'm male. Isn't that rather chauvinistic on your part?"

"Touché," she groaned. "All right, I'll go over it once, briefly. Do you have any idea what it's like to work for weeks on a major presentation to management and then have your boss introduce you to the assembled staff as 'Our very attractive Miss Cameron, who is as easy on the eye as she is on her expense account'? Not a word about the fact that I was one of the firm's top performers during the last two quarters or that I'd closed a deal everyone else had thought was lost forever. Prescott would never have dared introduce his highest-achieving male employee in such a way. It would have been ludicrous and demeaning, to say the least. But he didn't think twice about doing it to me. Then there were all those cocktail parties where I was supposed to ignore his arm around my shoulders and the clever remarks about my 'seductive' salesmanship. How about the annual meeting last year when Prescott told his sales staff to get contacts the color of my eyes so they could try batting their lashes at the lady clients the way I did at the male clients? Then there were all those occasions when he called me girl. The males on the sales staff, of course, are always referred to as men. How about the time I lost my temper in a sales meeting and he asked me jokingly if it was 'that time of the month'? I've heard men lose their tempers in his meetings and everyone sits back respectfully. I do it one time and he says a thing like that! And let's not forget last month's company picnic when he . . ."

Gage flung up a hand. "All right, all right. I get the picture. A lot of little things that add up over a period of time. Did you try explaining that to him? Aaron Prescott's not exactly stupid."

"Of course I did, and that's when he made all those accusations. He's the kind of man who will never understand how offensive he is to professional women. There's no point trying to explain it to him because he's thoroughly set in his ways. He's of an old school of masculine behavior that will never change. He may not be stupid in business generally, but believe me he's thickheaded enough when it comes to business relationships!" Rani took another long swallow of her drink. Just reminding herself of all those little annoying instances was enough to elicit the old exasperation. She shouldn't have remained with Prescott Services as long as she had. She should have had sense enough to see that her career was always going to be limited there. Suddenly she became aware of Gage's thoughtful silence on the other side of the table. "Well? Whose side are you on?"

He gave her a very straight look. "It's not my position to judge. My job is to get you back to Dallas."

"For heaven's sake, why?" Rani exploded in a muffled tone. "I was a good account executive for the firm, but there are a lot of other good ones there, too. I assure you, Gage, I can be replaced. Why would Prescott want me back?"

"Reason number one," Gage informed her coolly, "is that you can't be replaced, apparently. At least not for securing the Henderson account."

Rani straightened, startled. "The Henderson account! But that was almost signed, sealed and delivered. What happened?" Prescott Services sold packages of various business, legal and financial services to its clients. For one monthly fee it supplied all the accounting, bookkeeping, inventory control routines, payroll services and other such necessary business procedures needed by large and small firms. The Henderson account was the last one Rani had been working on before she left. She had turned it over to a co-worker with full instructions on how to handle Mrs. Henderson, the widowed owner of Henderson Gourmet Markets.

"Mrs. Henderson, it seems, won't deal with anyone else but you. According to Aaron, she doesn't like being handed off to another account executive in the middle of negotiations."

"And Prescott Services is in danger of losing the whole deal?" Wide-eyed, Rani sat very still and considered the implications. The laughter began to build inside her until it threatened to erupt. But she managed to keep it contained for a few minutes longer as Gage continued.

"That's what I'm told. Prescott wants you back to conclude the deal. And that, I'm afraid, is only reason number one."

"Go on," she said breathlessly. "I can't wait to hear reason number two."

"Prescott's son, Brady, walked out in a huff, apparently, after he heard that you'd left. Claims he won't come back to the firm until you're back," Gage finished with suspicious lack of inflection.

"Oh, my God! This is priceless!" The laughter spilled over into a joyous, exuberant noise. "I couldn't have done better if I'd *tried!* I can't believe it! Prescott must be fit to be tied! A major client lost and the heir apparent storming out of the front office! It's perfect! Absolutely perfect!"

He let her recover from her delighted amusement, waiting patiently until the laughter had sunk back into giggles and she was wiping the tears from her eyes. "You mean you didn't plan it all?" he finally asked evenly.

"Of course not! How could I? I thought the Henderson account was in the bag and I thought Brady would have had more sense than to annoy his father to that extent. It would never have occurred to me to even attempt such a double-edged coup!" She shook her head, still grinning happily. "It just goes to show that there must be some justice in this world after all. Prescott will at least remember me. It's too much to hope that he'll treat his next female account executive any differently than he treated me, but maybe he'll wonder a little about where he went wrong. Who knows? If enough women walk out, he might even begin to think he's doing something wrong!"

Gage watched her expressionlessly as tamales and tacos were set before them. She couldn't tell what he was thinking, but Rani told herself she didn't much care. He'd already made it clear he was on Prescott's side. With a surge of appetite she picked up her fork and tackled a tamale.

"I'm afraid," he eventually said very gently as he slowly picked up his own fork, "that your revenge is going to have to be a little short-lived."

"Why?" She lifted her eyes and fixed him with an abruptly narrowed stare. "I'm not going back to clean up the mess, Gage. You'd better understand that right now."

He chewed reflectively before answering. "I'm going to have to insist on it," he finally murmured.

"Insist all you want, I wouldn't go back to Dallas for all the cows in Texas. What's in this for you, Gage?" she threw back, letting her scorn show clearly in her words as she challenged him point-blank. "Why are you getting involved?"

"I've given Prescott my word I'll take care of this situation for him," he said simply, sinking strong white teeth into a chunk of taco.

"Your word?" She pounced at once. "You mean Aaron Prescott is paying you to persuade me to return? This is a job for you?"

Something hard flickered in his eyes and was gone. "I told Prescott I'd handle this. He asked me to look into the matter and I agreed. That's all that you need to know." The taco disappeared in about three bites. A very large man.

"Do you do this sort of thing a lot in your business?" she demanded, fascinated.

"Chase after runaways? No, not a lot. This was something of a special instance. I've known Aaron Prescott for some time, you see."

"No, I don't see. What difference does knowing him make? Do you always do other people's dirty work for them?" The whiplash that appeared in her voice had its effect. His blue-gray eyes went very cold, and Rani found herself unexpectedly shivering.

"My reasons for taking on this particular task are none of your business, Rani. The only thing you need to keep in mind is that once I've accepted a job I always see it through to the end." He leaned forward, bracing his elbows on the table as he fixed her with a merciless stare. "Do you understand? I will take you back to Dallas, one way or another. It's up to you how pleasant or unpleasant a trip you wish to make."

She sucked in her breath, renewed fury battling the chill that had gone through her veins at the warning in his words. "Do you know what they used to call men like you in this part of the country?" she asked cuttingly. "Men who chased down other people for a reward? They called them bounty hunters, Gage Fletcher. Is that what you are? A bounty hunter? No questions asked, just do your job and get paid?"

"It's a living," he drawled dangerously.

"Is it indeed? And do you have orders to take me in dead or alive?"

"You're in luck," he retorted a little too kindly. "You're only good to me alive."

Rani was on her feet before he'd finished the sentence. Eyes flashing with the gold of her thoroughly aroused temper, she leaned over and flattened her palms on the table. Gage didn't move, returning her gaze with an even, controlled stare that underlined his own confidence in the outcome of the confrontation as nothing else could have done.

"Listen, *messenger boy*," she said intently, "you can take this message to Prescott. Tell him I have no intention of going back to clean things up. Tell him I hope he loses the Henderson account altogether and tell him I hope Brady joins the French Foreign Legion. And tell him that if he sends any other bounty hunters after me, I'll sue him for harrassment!"

Then she turned on her heel and started for the door of the restaurant. Even though she was moving swiftly, however, she still caught Gage's last growl of sardonic warning. She had been meant to catch it.

"Discipline, Rani. Always remember: Discipline. You're going to lose the war without it, you know."

2

~~~~~~~~~~~~~~~~~~

The white Lincoln, heavily ornamented with chrome and complete with a personalized license plate that read "King," waited in the condominium drive as its owner said good night to Rani. Kingston Tanner looked a little like his car, Rani had decided earlier that day when he had arrived to pick her up for a promised horseback ride and barbequed rib dinner. Tall, blue-eyed and sandy-haired, King had an aura of twentieth-century wealth about him that told of financial interests in ranching, mining and natural gas. That evening he was even wearing the same colors as his car: a white, western-cut suit, white boots and hat and a silver-studded belt.

It had been a full day for Rani and it had gotten off to a bad start with a long ride aboard a horse named QE2. The animal had, indeed, seemed almost as large as the luxury liner for which it had been named. It had been well behaved, which was a vast relief to Rani, who had spent very little time on anything other than carousel horses, but the long ride through the foothills of the

Sandia Mountains had been almost too much for her. She had arrived back at the Tanner ranch incredibly stiff and sore but far too polite to let her host know just how much she was suffering.

After changing into a flounced prairie skirt and a full-sleeved white blouse trimmed in lace, she had been escorted through the large, rambling Tanner home to a backyard barbeque attended by several of King's neighbors. Forced to eat a great deal more food than she normally consumed at one sitting and to carry on a conversation about cattle futures on the commodities market, Rani was drained and drooping by the time she had at last persuaded King to take her home.

But there they were at last, standing in her doorway. King hadn't been too happy about bringing her all the way back to Albuquerque so late at night. He had been hoping she would stay at the ranch. Now that he had made the trip, however, he was beginning to hint at an alternative solution for spending the remainder of the evening.

"Heck, I could just bunk down right there in your livin' room, darlin'. No problem at all," he assured her with a boyish enthusiasm Rani knew better than to trust.

Holding the jeans and shirt she had worn earlier for the horseback ride, Rani shook her head with smiling firmness. The best way to handle King Tanner was by gently manipulating his masculine ego. "Now, King, I don't think that would be a good idea at all," she drawled, wincing inwardly as she realized how her normally mild southwestern twang deepened considerably after she'd spent a few hours in Tanner's company. "It would just be asking for trouble. The thought of you right out there in my living room for a whole night might be a little too much for me and you know it!" Actually, Rani admitted to herself, the real problem was that the thought of his sleeping under the same roof with her wouldn't be too much at all. Nice as King was, he did not set her pulses racing or make her wonder about what it would be like to spend the night in his arms. If he were to sleep on her couch, she wouldn't find herself tempted in the least. The knowledge depressed her.

But King was grinning, pleased, as she looked up at him through her lashes. "Darlin', I don't rightly see that as a problem," he chuckled easily. "At least not a problem I couldn't handle."

"I'll just bet you could handle it! Why in the world do you think I'm sending you on your way home? Off you go, King Tanner. You have wined and dined and dazzled me enough for one day. I need time to recover!" Her smile was warm enough and real enough. She really did like the man. To give King his due, his intentions were quite honorable, but she wouldn't make a good wife for him.

He was forty years old and widowed, with two young children. Tanner wanted a wife who could adapt to ranch life and raise his sons to inherit the empire he was building. The more Rani dated him, the more certain she was that he was beginning to think of her as a potential wife and mother. Soon she would have to gently break off the relationship. King Tanner believed in love and he deserved a woman who could truly love him.

He kissed her then, taking his dismissal with good grace, and Rani tried very hard to find something special in King's embrace. It was pleasant enough, rather like the man himself, but having reached the age of thirty-two and having enjoyed an active social life, Rani had known others that were equally pleasant. Why was it that the older she grew, the more easily dissatisfied and demanding she became with the men she dated?

King was a perfect mate for her in many ways, Rani thought wryly as she closed the door on his reluctantly departing figure. Her relationship with him had been serene and comfortable. But then, all of her relationships with men were serene and comfortable or she ended them very quickly.

Serenity and calm and gentleness were the qualities she demanded in a man, yet every time she found them she seemed to grow dissatisfied. Somehow she grew restless and bored, a part of her seeking something else, something she couldn't name, even to herself.

It made her uneasy even to think about what might be lacking in her relationships with men. The words *passion* and *excitement* might describe what it was that she missed by sticking to safe, comfortable men, but they also conjured up images of the turbulent, unsettling male-female conflict that had been so much a part of her parents' marriage. Those images had haunted too many nights of a little girl who couldn't sleep through what seemed near-violent screaming battles conducted after the children were in bed. Sometimes those battles had begun even before Rani and her sister had been sent off to their rooms.

As she grew older she was convinced with each new conflict between her parents that divorce was imminent. She had learned to live in dread of the day when she and her sister would be taken aside and given the frightening news.

Yet, that day had never come. The violence of the quarreling had usually evaporated the day after the battle. To that day her parents were still married, and although the battles were far less frequent, Rani knew they could still be just as loud and alarming to an onlooker. It was only as she grew older that she had begun to recognize the deep passion between her parents, which not only gave rise to the conflict but also put an end to each battle. But that degree of passion was something that still frightened her. She had resolved before she was out of her teens never to become involved in a relationship that resembled that of her parents. The little-girl fears had never quite died.

But that didn't mean she didn't long for love in a softer, safer form. King Tanner would be able to provide the kind of love she wanted, Rani told herself. He was a nice man who would always take care of her. In return he would expect a well-run home and children.

He also had the right to expect a reasonable degree of love and physical affection in bed, and Rani knew she would have a hard time faking that for the next fifty years.

It would also be damn hard to learn to fake a love of horseback riding, she thought with a grimace as she slowly began to undress. She had been aching all afternoon from the effects of the QE2. The effort of being relaxed and scintillating during the rest of the day for the sake of her host and his guests had been too much. What she really needed was a long soak in the whirlpool spa that was one of the amenities of the condominium complex.

With abrupt decision Rani reached into a drawer for a silver-gray maillot swimsuit. Stepping out of her prairie skirt, she changed quickly and then stuck a few more hairpins into the loosening coil of hair on top of her head. She hoped they would control the tendrils that were always threatening to spill down around her shoulders. Yanking a huge gold towel out of the hall closet, she walked outside through the kitchen door, which opened onto the large communal lawn and garden. In the center, beneath a latticework gazebo, the heated spa waited. Flipping on the switch that set the jets of water in motion, Rani slipped into the bubbling hot water with a soft sigh of relief.

She had brought a small cassette player out with her, and now she set the little machine carefully on the edge of the pool and fitted the earphones over her head. Pressing the button she closed her eyes and gave herself over to the soft, pummeling water and the strains of a Mozart flute concerto. Overhead a canopy of black velvet and silver stars sealed the night around her. It must be nearly midnight, Rani realized absently.

She tried to imagine King on his way home. He would

be halfway there by now. A nice man and a successful one. What more could a woman ask? But try as she might, Rani knew she would never feel a genuine need for him or even a genuine level of excitement.

Actually, annoying though the knowledge was, the only exciting male in her life recently was Gage Fletcher. Mouth twisting wryly at the thought, Rani shifted her legs languidly beneath the foaming water and inclined her head back against the edge of the pool. The wonderfully controlled exuberance of the concerto seemed to fill the world.

What had the man done after she'd walked out of the restaurant the day before? Had he done as she'd instructed and obediently carried her message back to Aaron Prescott? It was hard to imagine Gage as a mere messenger boy. It was hard to imagine him at anyone's beck and call, in fact. On the other hand, she *could* conceive of him allowing nothing to stand in the way of finishing a job he had contracted to perform.

Rani frowned to herself at the thought. So how would such a man react if a stumbling block had been firmly placed in his path? She had half expected him to contact her again that day. That was one of the reasons she'd been glad of King's invitation to the ranch. It had neatly gotten her out of the vicinity. Had Gage come by her house or gone to the shop? Would he pursue the matter further? No doubt about it, he had managed to make his presence felt in her life. There she was, fresh from King's good-night kiss, dwelling on Gage Fletcher's possible actions! King would be chagrined if he ever discovered that.

In her mind, Rani refought the Battle of Hastings as the flute concerto flowed through her head. What would have happened if Harold's men had stood firm instead of charging down the hill in hot pursuit and leaving themselves exposed to William's cavalry? What would have happened if she had stood firm behind the counter of The Miniature World instead of charging out the door in pursuit of the man who had deliberately baited her out into the open?

Well, it hadn't done Gage any good, she reminded herself with great satisfaction, and it had given her some very interesting information. Aaron Prescott was feeling the pinch of her absence! Served the man right. That thought made her wonder how Gage would tell his employer of his failure. It wouldn't be easy for him to do. She had the feeling Gage Fletcher seldom failed at anything. There was a controlled power and masculine certainty that seemed to emanate from him. Such power and certainty rarely admitted to failure.

It wasn't until the flute concerto was abruptly cut off and strong male fingers lifted the earphones away from her head that Rani realized with a shock that she was not alone under the gazebo. Reacting with startled instinct and propelled by a genuine shaft of fear, she whirled in the foaming water, backing automatically toward the opposite edge of the pool.

"Gage!"

"It would seem the noble King left a little too soon, or didn't you invite him to share your bath?" Gage asked, braced on one knee by the edge of the spa. The hand holding the earphones rested on the other knee. Wearing jeans and a shirt that appeared nearly black in the dim light, he seemed unexpectedly dark and intimidating.

It struck Rani at that moment that King had definitely been wearing the color of the good guys that evening. Even the Lincoln had been white. Gage, on the other hand, was all shadow and menace. For some crazy reason she found herself remembering that his Jag had been sleek and black.

"What in heaven's name are you doing here?" she snapped, hoping the shakiness in her voice wasn't apparent. "Have you been spying on me, Gage? It won't do any good, you know. Nothing you do will make me go back to Dallas with you! And it isn't just Prescott I'll be suing if you don't leave me alone!"

"Come on, Rani," he chided quite gently, "you didn't expect me to give up just because you walked out on me yesterday at the restaurant, did you? I told you I always finish a job. The way I see it, our war has just begun. I realize now there may be a number of small skirmishes before the decisive battle."

She lifted her chin in arrogant disdain, vaguely aware that she was no longer feeling tired or drained. New energy had begun to pulse through her. Energy that could not be entirely explained by the effects of the spa and the concerto. Her hands made idle, sweeping motions beneath the surface of the water as she eyed her opponent. "What's the matter, Gage? Don't you get paid unless you bring me back? Won't Prescott reimburse you for time and expenses unless you're successful?"

"The question doesn't arise. I intend to be successful."

Rani began to smile slowly, mockingly. In the shadowy light it was almost possible to see the gleam of gold in her eyes. "There is nothing you can do or say, Gage, to make me surrender."

"You don't know that," he countered. "I haven't tried a fraction of the weapons in my arsenal."

"Which one are you going to try tonight?" she dared.

"Logic. It can be very effective when one is dealing with a reasonably intelligent adversary. I've been led to believe you do qualify as reasonably intelligent," he added obliquely, giving her a fraction of a grin that revealed a slash of white teeth.

"You shouldn't believe everything you're told, Gage. But go on, do your worst. Let's hear the logic."

He watched her in musing silence for a long moment, as if considering carefully how to begin. Then he said deliberately, "Prescott is not without influence, Rani. Have you given any thought to how he could jeopardize your future career if you anger him? When you find a new job you're going to need references, recommendations, a good track record. Prescott could punish you very thoroughly by denying you all of that. He has power in his circles here in the Southwest. He came up the hard way and he knows how to use muscle."

Rani blinked. Prescott was a potential threat only if she were to stay in the same field of business, she reminded herself silently. What Prescott and Gage didn't know, of course, was that she had no intention of going back into the same line of work. The decision to buy her sister's shop had been crystallizing in her mind for months and had become a firm reality after she'd made the break with Prescott Services, Inc. That decision, she now realized, was an effective secret weapon.

"Sorry," she murmured lightly, "I can't bring myself to be suitably terrified. Any more logic?"

He studied her. "I'm serious, Rani. I've known Aaron Prescott for several years. He can be quite ruthless. Three years ago he hired me to find out who was leaking confidential financial information about his clients to rival firms. I found the guy and gave Prescott the details he needed to make a reasonable case for firing him. But he decided to make an example of the culprit. He didn't just fire him, he let it be known that if any other firm took on his ex-employee, he'd go to the press with publicity that would make the hiring firm look as if it had been involved in the industrial espionage. Believe me, no one employee was worth that amount of trouble to any rival firm here in the Southwest. And that wasn't the end of it. Prescott knew the guy had a loan application in at a bank in Houston. Apparently the man had planned to build a house with some of his ill-gotten gains. One call from Prescott to the loan officer was enough to ruin his chances of getting the loan. Rani, Prescott didn't just get rid of an employee who had been disloyal, he made it impossible for that man to continue living and working in this part of the country! Do you understand what I'm saying? He won't allow you to get away with your revenge. He'll punish you very thoroughly if you try it! He'll make an example of you."

In spite of her plans for the future, Rani felt a distinct

shiver of apprehension go down her spine. "He'd go to that kind of trouble just because I refuse to come back and close the Henderson account?"

"It's a little more complicated than that and you know it. Brady might be persuaded to come back to the home front after his rebellion has cooled, but if you take the Henderson account to your next employer . . ." He let the sentence trail off as his full meaning dawned on Rani.

"So that's it!" she exclaimed, thoroughly amused now. "Prescott's worried that I'll try to buy my way into my next job with the Henderson business. What a brilliant idea! I must give it some thought!"

"And Brady?" Gage muttered dryly.

"I think you're right about Brady," she acknowledged with a rueful smile. "He's got some noble aspirations, but basically his future is tied to his father's desk and he knows it. He'll be back sooner or later." It was the truth. Brady Prescott was a likeable young man who had graduated from a very enlightened university business school. He had understood Rani's situation and had disapproved of his father's behavior more than once, but she hadn't really expected him to do something as dramatic as walking out in protest. There had been nothing more personal between her and Brady than a friendship based on their similar ages and academic backgrounds. Did Prescott realize that or was he wondering if Brady had dashed off to Albuquerque, too? Matters were becoming more interesting and amusing by the moment.

"I assume from that smile on your face that my logic isn't making much headway," Gage said flatly.

"I guess I'm just not in the mood for it," she chuckled.

"We're talking about something that could affect your whole future, Rani," he told her bluntly.

"That's my problem, not yours."

"Then I suggest you start worrying about it!"

"Thank you for your concern, but I'm afraid I can't overlook the fact that your advice is generated more by your desire to do your job than to protect me," she said sweetly. "Tell me, how did you find me here in the whirlpool? Were you spying on me?"

"You've been gone most of the day. I was beginning to think you wouldn't be back this evening at all," he replied slowly.

"Have you bugged my bedroom with some of your security devices?" she goaded.

"There's not much need, is there?" he countered. "Poor King got a rather short good night at your door a little while ago."

"You were watching?" Indignation flared at the realization. "Of all the despicable, sneaky, underhanded things to do! You should be ashamed of yourself!"

He drew a long breath. "I had to know what the situation was between the two of you."

"Why?" she snapped furiously. "Afraid I might drag him into the battle on my side? It wouldn't be a bad notion. King has money and power. I wouldn't hesitate to put him up against Aaron Prescott any day!"

"It isn't Prescott he'll be up against," Gage pointed out calmly. "I'm the one he'd have to face first. And something tells me you won't ask him to take that risk."

"What makes you think that I wouldn't?" She breathed tightly, knowing with sickening sureness that he was quite right.

"Because you wouldn't ask a man to fight your battles for you unless you were prepared to commit yourself to him in return. I got the feeling from what I saw tonight that you're a long way from committing yourself to King Tanner. Which means you'll be fighting your own war, doesn't it, Rani?"

"For a messenger boy you're making a lot of assumptions!" she lashed back, infuriated at the accuracy of those assumptions.

"But I'm not just the messenger, Rani, and you know it," he retorted steadily. "I'm the battlefield commander Prescott has selected."

"Just how much is he paying you for this, Gage?" she taunted harshly.

There was a dangerous stillness about him as he met her eyes. "Does it matter?"

Definitely his weak spot, Rani told herself with satisfaction. Gage Fletcher didn't want to discuss his own motivation for accepting this job. She zeroed in on that weakness with grim satisfaction.

"Just curiosity. One does wonder how much one is worth in a situation like this," she murmured. "I must say, I'm impressed with Prescott's ability to snap his fingers and have you at his beck and call. I was merely wondering what the going rate is for this sort of thing. Who knows? I might want to hire you myself sometime in the future. Or someone like you. If I paid you enough money, Gage, would you run and fetch for me?"

The stillness in his kneeling frame had been the quiet before the storm. Before she understood exactly what was happening, Gage seemed to explode into action. He moved, stretching out one square hand across the churning water to grasp her around the back of the neck.

Rani started to struggle, but everything happened much too quickly. She was being dragged out of the water and up onto the edge of the small spa before she could even utter a half-strangled protest.

"Gage! Stop it! What do you think you're doing?"

Then she was on her feet and the gold towel was wrapped once around her water-slick body. Still the hand at the back of her neck gripped her as if she were a kitten, holding her in place, and then she was being hauled against Gage's massive strength.

Stunned at the rush of events, Rani lifted her gaze in wide-eyed protest, her lips parting for the stream of abuse she intended to hurl. But the words were stopped in her throat as his mouth came down on hers.

"The fee I'd charge you for doing your running and fetching has nothing to do with money!" he grated roughly against her lips. Then his arms were around her, crushing her into his warmth while his mouth sought to dominate hers completely.

The controlled explosion of his power was translated into a kiss that was wholly unlike anything Rani had ever experienced. It seemed to pour itself into her, swamping her senses and wiping out the fleeting thought of resistance. Rani sagged beneath the shock wave of the embrace, her body leaning into Gage's strength for support.

His mouth moved on hers with electrifying intensity, and she knew instinctively that the initial assault was meant to stun her responses. There was a damp heat in the contact of their lips that flowed through her like lightning. Locked to him by arms of sinewy power, her senses swirling about her in the darkness, Rani let her lips flower open to admit the surging thrust of Gage's tongue. She seemed to have no choice.

With a muffled groan he acknowledged the victory, seeking out the taste and feel of her inner warmth. Then her own tongue was located and coerced into an intimate battle that was incredibly exhilarating. She began to fight back for the sheer excitement of the skirmish. Unaware of what she was doing, her hands lifted to the broad shoulders of the man who held her so tightly, and her nails began to sink into the dark fabric of his shirt. The silvered coral tint at the tips of her fingers was a savage splash of color against the garment.

He must have recognized the passion he had ignited within her because his own seemed to be taking quantum jumps. Rani was certain the kiss had begun as a form of retaliation, but she knew beyond a shadow of a doubt that they were both caught up in it now.

Dear God, there hadn't been even a fraction of this elemental excitement and need in King's good-night embrace. Rani hadn't known anything like this in her life! Greedily, with the overpowering hunger of a starving woman who has just been presented a banquet, Rani gave herself up to Gage's kiss. She would sort out all the ramifications later. Right now there was only the night and this all-consuming man.

With great reluctance Gage pulled away from her lips at last, searching out the vulnerable, sensitive line of her throat. "Rani, Rani, what are you doing to me?" he muttered hoarsely.

She didn't answer. She couldn't answer. In that moment she only wanted to lose herself in the flames he had sparked. Her arms wrapped around his neck as he buried one hand in the knot of her hair and eased her head back. She shivered at the touch of his mouth against her throat, her pulses beginning to hammer. Eyes tightly closed against the thrill of the moment, she moaned softly.

Then his hands shifted again, finding the upper edge of the strapless maillot.

"Gage," she whispered, shaken, as his fingers slid beneath the tight-fitting silver-gray fabric of the swimsuit. But he stopped her faint protest, drinking his name from her lips even as she spoke.

She gasped as the exciting roughness of his hands slid down the sides of her body, drawing the top half of the suit to her waist in a swift movement. The towel fell away completely to wind up in a pool of gold at their feet. Then he was lifting his head, his eyes meeting hers as she looked up at him through lowered lashes. Holding her gaze, he raised his palms with tantalizing slowness up from her waist. She trembled beneath his touch, her lips parted, eyes full of passion and wondrous uncertainty.

The depths of his own desire blazed back at her from his gray eyes. And in those depths she saw as great a degree of wonder as she felt in herself. Whatever Gage Fletcher had intended when he'd begun the kiss, it was not this ensnaring desire that was claiming them both. Knowing he was as unexpectedly trapped in it as she, Rani was able to enjoy the moment. Her fingertips stroked his wide shoulders and then curled deeply into the sable darkness of his hair. The crisp thickness of it was fascinating to her senses.

The warm palms at her waist had risen almost to the level of her breasts, and she could feel the shudder that went through Gage as he hesitated a fraction longer and then closed his fingers gently around the small curving globes.

"Oh, Gage!" Rani's breath hissed between her teeth as she shut her eyes once more and leaned into him, hiding her face against his chest. There she inhaled the earthy male scent of him and quivered again.

"Sweetheart," he growled against the fallen array of her hair, "the feel of you is driving me out of my mind. You have the body of a cat. Slender and so damn sensuous. I can feel your nipples hardening under my hand. Do you know what it's doing to me?"

"Tell me," she urged breathlessly, needing to hear the exciting words.

"I want to put you down here on the grass, finish removing this damn swimsuit and then take you so completely you would never be able to look at another man. God, woman! I want to ravish you, do you realize that?"

There was so much self-astonishment in his voice that Rani's excitement became tinged with a feminine indulgence she had never experienced before. Gage certainly had never intended the punishing kiss to lead to this!

"Ravishment isn't quite what I had in mind," she whispered throatily, raising her head to meet his searing gaze. "But a few more kisses . . . ?" She let the words trail off invitingly, expectantly.

His reaction was not at all what she was expecting, however. The steel in him was suddenly very evident. She felt it in the thighs that thrust against hers and saw it in the harsh line of his jaw. His rough palms moved with slow intent on her nipples, causing her breasts to swell and grow even more taut.

"Do you really believe I could stand here and trade a few more kisses in the moonlight and then call it quits?" he demanded raggedly. "I want to take you, Rani Cameron, not flirt with you. There's one hell of a difference. Don't count on me to play by the same rules of war Tanner seems willing to obey."

She heard the masculine warning in his voice and still had enough sense left to heed it. Gage was telling her the raw truth. He wasn't going to be content to sample a little more of this incredible excitement they had discovered. He would want it all. And God help her! He'd have her wanting the same thing, Rani told herself dazedly as she gingerly tried to put a little distance between them.

As she stepped away from him, however, her breasts were exposed fully to his gaze. The hands on her nipples fell away slowly, but the touch of his eyes was every bit as tangible. Hastily Rani reached down for the gold towel and wrapped it around herself. What had gotten into her? Less than an hour before she had been telling herself that this kind of passion probably didn't exist for her!

"Rani!"

She looked at him, drawn by the husky sound of her name on his lips. "No, Gage. I'll admit you took me by surprise, but I'm not going to go to bed with you. You're my enemy, remember?" she concluded whimsically as she clutched the towel safely around her naked breasts.

He shook his head once in a sharp negative. "That's what I want to set straight," he said carefully. "Whatever else happens between us, this side of things isn't involved. Do you understand?"

She stared at him. "I don't see how it can be separated from the rest. You only want one thing from me, Gage: my agreement to go back to Dallas so that you can do your job and collect your payment. I would be a fool to let you seduce me, wouldn't I? Business and pleasure don't mix."

Reaching out, he clasped his hands around her bare shoulders, holding her still. "We can and will separate it!

When we go to bed together, Rani, there will be only the two of us involved. It will have nothing to do with my job or your stubbornness on other matters!"

"*When* we go to bed!" she repeated, outraged. "You mean *if*, don't you? And it's a very large *if*, I assure you!"

"I think we can say it's a certainty," he drawled more gently. "But whatever happens, when the time comes, remember what I've said. Give me your word on that, sweetheart. Please."

He meant it, she realized. He really meant it. Gage fully intended to keep the matter of their physical attraction for each other outside the realm of the other battle in which they were engaged. Was such a thing possible? And if she told herself it was possible, could she then resist the lure of him?

Bravely she met the demand in him with her own challenge, striving to keep her voice flippant. "I'm not the one who needs to understand the ground rules. You're the one who has to get something straight, Gage. Seducing me would not get you one step closer to achieving your goal of taking me back to Dallas. Is that very clear?"

He nodded at once, which surprised her. "I accept that. Now give me your word that you'll let whatever happens between us personally remain just that—between us. It stays off the battlefield."

"But of course, Gage," Rani managed very sweetly, turning to head back toward her condominium. "I wouldn't think of making love on a battlefield. So unromantic!"

3

〰〰〰〰〰〰〰〰

It was the pounding on her front door that woke her early the next morning. Rani blinked sleepily, stirred amidst the peach-colored sheets and buried her head deeper into the pillow in an effort to pretend that the pounding was being conducted on her neighbor's door.

But the relentless noise continued with the sort of steady beat that said whoever was causing the racket didn't intend to give up and disappear. With a groan, she struggled to the edge of the bed, bronze hair tumbling around her shoulders in its usual early-morning chaos. She glared in the direction of the closet until a paisley robe came into focus. Struggling out of bed, Rani reached for it, belting the comfortable, ruffle-necked, long-sleeved garment around her slender waist. Sliding her feet into fluffy slippers, she headed at last for the door.

When she reached it she didn't hesitate, throwing it open with an annoyed look on her face. "It's six o'clock in the morning," she began rudely. "What the hell do you want?"

Gage's dark brows came together in an admonishing glance as he stood staring down at her sleep-softened figure. "You shouldn't open the door until you've established who's on the other side, Rani."

"I do not need lectures on security from you at this hour of the morning, even if you are an expert. Save them for your clients," she grumbled. "Besides, I knew it was you. No one else would have the nerve to wake me at this hour!"

"Not at your best at six in the morning?" He moved into the hall, not waiting for an invitation. Disgruntled and not at all sure how to stop him, Rani fell back in retreat.

"I'm not at my best, whatever that may amount to, until after I've showered and had my coffee," she declared forcefully. She continued hopefully, "Come back in a couple of hours and—"

"And you'll be gone," he concluded. "I talked to your sister yesterday when I couldn't find you here and she said you were going to be managing the shop today."

Rani slid him a probing glance, trying to determine what else Donna might have told him. Had her sister said anything about Rani buying The Miniature World in a couple of months? For some reason she couldn't yet explain, Rani wanted to keep that bit of information in reserve. All intelligent battle commanders tried to maintain a little something in reserve, she decided. She would speak to Donna the first chance she got and ask her not to mention the impending sale of the shop.

"I don't go down to the shop until around nine-thirty," she said, not knowing quite what to do now that the man was inside her home. He seemed rather large, standing there in the hall. "Donna needs some time off to arrange for wedding pictures."

"Is this your sister's first marriage? From what she said yesterday it's going to be a large affair." Gage was beginning to glance interestedly around the apartment.

"Her second. The first one was a disaster. She was only nineteen at the time and the guy wasn't much older. She was divorced by the time she was twenty-one. They eloped," Rani explained, starting toward the kitchen with the intention of at least putting on some coffee for herself. "Donna always vowed that if she married again, she'd take her time and do it right. This wedding's going to have all the trappings the first one lacked, plus a nice long engagement. My sister is having a great time with it, but I think poor Lou is about at his wit's end!" She picked up a can of coffee and began worrying the lid.

"Lou being the groom?"

"Ummm. A very patient man, I must say. I suppose you want some coffee?" she remarked ungraciously.

"I'll fix it while you go take your shower," he drawled, a smile edging his firm mouth as he took the canister of coffee out of her hand. "You look a little too inclined to poison me. Run along, sweetheart," he added in a patient manner as she hesitated suspiciously. "I'm not going to assault you this morning. I'm here on business."

"You're going to fire the next weapon in your arsenal?" In spite of her flippancy, Rani felt a tinge of uneasiness. She kept telling herself that nothing this man did would have any effect on her decision not to go back to Dallas, but there was no denying both the physical strength and the willpower of Gage Fletcher. His determination to succeed was intimidating in itself.

"I certainly am. Why else do you think I got here almost at dawn?"

"Hoping to catch the enemy sleeping and undefended?" she shot back sweetly.

"Dawn raids are often the most successful kind. Go take your shower, Rani. You know you're curious about what I'll try next."

Chin up in haughty denial, Rani started out of the kitchen, only to have her wrist snagged. Startled, she swung back to face Gage. "You said you weren't here to assault me!" she began in automatic protest as he lowered his head to take her lips.

"Think of this as a salute before battle," he muttered. "I can't resist." He kissed her with a lazy thoroughness that held only a hint of the previous night's overwhelming passion and then he let her go.

Once again Rani beat a hasty retreat, allowing herself to acknowledge for the first time that she half wished Gage hadn't left so obediently the evening before. But he had, after walking her back to her door. He'd relinquished his hold on her without any argument and simply melted back into the night from which he had come. Rani had told herself that that was the way she wanted it, but even then she'd been lying.

As she stepped beneath the shower's spray she allowed herself to remember fully just how enthralled she had been in his arms. Never had her body reacted with such instinctive passion. She couldn't understand how it had arisen out of the argument they had been having, but it had seemed to explode into life the moment he had reached for her. Was this how it had been between her parents? That thought made her more uneasy than she had ever been in her life. She wanted no part of a relationship that resembled that of her parents!

But this was different, Rani consoled herself. Her association with Gage existed solely because of the business that lay between them. And Rani had never had any objection to holding her own on the battlefield of business. Indeed, her hard work and determination to succeed in a man's world had more than once thrown her into conflict with outdated male prejudice and chauvinism. That she could handle. That kind of battle was safe because it never involved the emotional or passionate side of her nature.

She told herself the conflict with Gage was a business conflict, one she could handle. Yet, how could she deny the way the battle had leaped from the business barricades to a far more intimate firefight the night before, when he had taken her in his arms?

If only there weren't this other matter between them. If only he weren't a paid bounty hunter sworn to bring her back to Dallas so he could make good on his word to Prescott. If only he weren't deliberately laying siege to her. If only . . .

She thought again of his injunction the previous night. Did he really believe they could separate the physical side of their relationship from the war they were conducting? And where did that leave her? In the middle of a full-scale affair with Gage Fletcher.

An affair with Gage. The thought was strangely alarming. It brought with it visions of passion accompanied by equally intense images of conflict. It was not the kind of relationship she had ever sought. Nor, she admitted reluctantly, had it ever been offered in quite that way. Why was it that at her age she was dangerously intrigued by such a man?

There was no question of love being involved, she warned herself. No pretense of it on either side. How could there be? They had only met a couple of days earlier and they were at odds over the Prescott business. That matter wasn't going to neatly disappear no matter how much Gage wanted to pretend it could be relegated to another battlefield. One could have an affair with one's enemy, Rani decided grimly, but one didn't fall in love with him.

But she was thirty-two years old and she had been protecting herself so long from the kind of relationship Gage promised that Rani was beginning to wonder what she had missed in the process of being so careful.

"My God, woman!" she chided herself in front of the mirror. "You're turning into a little old lady at the age of thirty-two. Soon you'll have to go out and buy yourself a cat for company."

A little old bachelor lady. What a depressing thought.

She made a face at herself in the mirror and then smiled wryly as she turned away to pull on her jeans and a red-and-white-striped shirt. She might be set in her ways, but they were comfortable, ordered ways. She was content with her life for the most part, and the decision to go into business for herself promised to smooth out the one area of her world that had been subject to conflict.

Until the previous night she had begun to think she was never fated to feel the incredible sensation of melting in a man's arms. Now, at last, she had been given a taste of that dangerous knowledge and had found that it didn't come free. The price tag attached promised a high cost. Uncertainty, conflict, tension and emotional danger on a level she had never before experienced.

For so long she had been avoiding that price.

"Rani! Coffee's ready. Want me to bring you a cup while you dress?"

"I'll be right out, Gage!" she called back, hastening down the hall toward the kitchen. Her step was suddenly full of the inner energy her thoughts had generated. She felt as if she were on the brink of an absolutely momentous decision, and the electricity of it shone in her eyes and put a warm color in her cheeks.

"You were right," Gage observed as she rounded the corner into the sunny kitchen. "A morning shower does do wonders for you. I can't wait to see what the coffee achieves!"

She smiled at him, taking the mug he was holding out. "I'm ready for battle. What are you going to hurl at me this morning?" The coffee was rich and very strong. "Don't tell me, let me guess. Is this coffee your secret weapon? It could sink a battleship!"

"Sorry," he apologized meekly. "I've been living on my own so long, I sometimes forget that not everyone drinks it this way. Want some cream in it?"

"I think so," she said, trying one more powerful swallow before giving up. She opened the refrigerator door and industriously searched out a carton of half-and-half. "Living on your own," she repeated as nonchalantly as possible. "You're not married?" First things first. She had to know exactly where she stood. If the price tag on Gage Fletcher included the cost of being the "other" woman, she would not even consider paying it.

"No," he told her softly. "I'm not married." She could feel his presence looming large behind her and knew there was more to come. "I doubt that I'd make any woman a good husband, Rani."

Well! That was fair warning, she thought as she poured the half-and-half into her mug. He had the grace, at least, to warn her not to misread his intentions. Coolly she shoved the carton back into the refrigerator, shut the door and turned to face him with a brilliant smile. "That makes us equal," she stated calmly, determined not to be outdone. She could be just as cool and modern and avant garde as he was. "I don't think I would make any man a very good wife."

A curious tension hovered in the air between them as they both assimilated the meaning behind their words. It was as if they had made an effort to get the ground rules out into the open. But Gage, it seemed, wanted to probe further.

"Because you don't feel you could remain faithful to one man?" There was a faint menace beneath the words. He would be a jealous lover, Rani thought wonderingly. For however long the relationship lasted, he would expect and demand faithfulness. And heaven help the woman who didn't obey his rules!

Rani lifted her chin, a fierce pride making her determined to maintain an aura of sophisticated nonchalance. "It has more to do with the fact that I'm rather content by myself. Set in my ways, I'm afraid. And I no longer get starry-eyed about that mystical concept known as love. I imagine it would be difficult now trying to make the adaptations necessary for marriage."

And, she suddenly realized, it would be much more dangerous. The thought of an affair with a man like Gage

Fletcher was unsettling enough. The thought of marriage truly terrified her. After all, presumably one could always walk away from an affair that grew too tempestuous and traumatizing to handle. But the commitment of marriage would be much harder to break. She looked up and found him watching her intently, his expression unreadable. "What about you, Gage? What makes you think you wouldn't make a good husband?"

He moved slowly across the room to sprawl in one of the chairs around the small kitchen table. "A variety of reasons. I'm nearly thirty-six years old and I think that love is mostly an illusion. I can understand desire and passion and need, but love? Well, that's for fantasy-spinning females. And females who want marriage want that fantasy. I'm unwilling to fake it for the sake of pleasing a woman. Even if I tried, it wouldn't last and it wouldn't be fair to her. Everyone has a right to his or her own dreams, but it would be wrong to pretend I was looking at the world through the same pair of rose-colored glasses. I prefer my relationships to be honest. And I suppose that, like you, I'm rather set in my ways now. I have no desire to start changing my life-style in order to cater to the whims and demands of a wife."

Rani managed a slow smile, although it was an effort. "A couple of crusty old bachelors and we haven't even gotten past forty yet. At least we should allow ourselves some of the pleasures of our advancing years. Are you hungry?"

"Starving," he confirmed with alacrity. "I told you I make it a point not to miss meals."

The truce lasted throughout breakfast, and neither one sought to disturb it by bringing up the subject of Gage's real reason for showing up at Rani's door at six in the morning. She would have to confront his next weapon soon enough, she told herself as they worked their way through hotcakes with honey and butter. For now she preferred to enjoy a respite from the warfare.

"Your sister mentioned yesterday that Tanner thinks

you'll make a good rancher's wife and I can see why," Gage remarked as he polished off the last of the hot-cakes. "You know how to cook and you go nicely with the southwestern look." This last remark was added with a meaningful glance at the interior decor of the condo-minium.

Rani decided to ignore the crack about King and shrugged instead. It was true. The condo, with its stylishly southwestern architectural features, suited her perfectly. There was a suggestion of the pueblo design in the beehive fireplace out in the living room. A luxuriously planted atrium lit by a skylight off the tiled entranceway reminded one of the cool, serene interior courtyards the Spanish had favored. The stucco-finished walls could have passed for adobe, and the windows were shaded and cool, allowing light without heat.

Throughout, Rani had dispersed the furniture and accessories she had been collecting for the past several years. Everything had been shipped back from Dallas on the same day she had left for Albuquerque, and now the western palette of colors warmed the rooms. Rich rusty oranges, the soft peach of a desert at dawn and the rich tones of the earth were displayed in her furniture and carpets. On the patio outside the kitchen sat a nineteenth-century Mexican settee. Indian baskets and Indian-inspired rugs decorated the halls. There was a comfortable, gracious feel to the place, and Gage was right. One really couldn't blame King for drawing his own conclusions from her surroundings. What the wealthy rancher failed to see was the overlay of city polish that glossed everything. It was not a working homestead. There was no room there for genuine mud or range dust. It was a stylish city condominium done with panache, and it would not have translated very easily to King's ranch home. King Tanner was viewing Rani and her background with the eyes of a man who thinks he's falling in love. Illusions.

The one item among Rani's furnishings that should

have given King the clue he needed caught Gage's eye
the moment he ambled out of the kitchen and into the
living room. The exquisitely designed Regency-style dollhouse was exhibited on a special table near the fireplace.
Behind it were shelves of books on the history of
dollhouse furnishings and Regency England interior design.

"It's incredible," Gage murmured, lowering himself in
front of the dollhouse to gaze into its many small rooms.
"Absolutely incredible. Did your sister give it to you?"

She smiled, drying her hands on a kitchen towel as she
came up behind him. It was an effort to resist the urge to
run her fingers through the darkness of his hair as she had
done the night before. Gage was wearing a white shirt
and a pair of dark slacks. A conservative dresser, she
decided in amusement. "I've had it for three years now.
When it arrived in Donna's shop, I couldn't resist. It's a
perfect Regency villa with curved window bays and tiny
balconies, complete with ironwork railings. Take a look at
the front," she urged. "It's even stuccoed, and there's a
little canopy."

"Amazing! But all the furnishings? Do you get them
through Donna?" Gage delicately fingered a small sculp-
tured figure that sat on a little claw-footed table.

"She keeps an eye out for the best things, and my
parents are always on the lookout, too."

"Your parents?" he questioned.

"Umm. They're in England on a tour at the moment.
They live in Houston."

"Mine live in San Diego. My father's a retired Navy
man. For some reason retired Navy officers always
gravitate toward San Diego," he said.

"How did you wind up in Albuquerque?"

He flicked her a short glance before going back to
studying the well-furnished miniature drawing room.
"My interest in military history has proven to be purely of
an intellectual orientation," he told her very dryly. "It
was soon evident to me that, in spite of my father's

fondest hopes, I wasn't going to make a career out of the military. I did my bit in Vietnam, but the blood was a little too real."

Rani caught her breath in quiet understanding. She sensed the tension in him as he spoke. "When I got out of the Army, which I had joined in a small gesture of rebellion toward my father, who wanted me in the Navy, I'd had enough of the real thing. I moved to Dallas and started my security consulting service and then, later, came here to Albuquerque."

"But you still have an academic interest in military history?" she questioned gently.

"I stick to pre–twentieth-century battles," he confessed grimly.

Rani nodded. "I can understand that. The twentieth-century stuff is far too real."

"Yes." He took her comprehension of that at face value. She understood.

He insisted on driving her to the shop and came inside with her while she opened up. Gage still hadn't returned to the subject of his next weapon, and while she was enjoying the truce, Rani was beginning to grow very, very curious. Was he delaying because he wasn't sure it would work or because he thought it might anger her? The idea that he didn't want to anger her was rather touching, she thought as she checked out the cash register.

Once she had prepared The Miniature World for a day of business, Rani turned her gaze to Gage.

"What are you doing?" she asked, seeing him seated in front of one of the tables used to display the military miniatures. He appeared deeply involved in the battle scene he was arranging.

"Do you mind if I set these up?" he asked absently, indicating a box of medieval French cavalry.

"No, of course not. They always sell better when they're displayed in action," she told him as she unlocked the front door. Then she wandered back to peer over his shoulder. "That's why I was setting up Hastings a couple of days ago. Donna always encourages me to handle the military miniatures whenever I'm in town. She finds it boring to read up on the individual battles."

"And if they're not displayed authentically, someone will point it out?" Gage grinned suddenly.

"The people who collect these things are sticklers for details," she admitted wryly. "Which battle are you doing?"

He sat back in his chair and smiled challengingly. "Pick a side and then I'll tell you."

"What? You mean you're not automatically going to stick me with the losers this time?" She studied the layout of archers and armored cavalry, trying to pinpoint the year if not the battle.

"Take your pick," Gage invited, sweeping a hand generously across the table.

"Given the fact that the French seem to outnumber the English by about three to one, I think I'll choose the French side," Rani chuckled obligingly. "No fair cheating if I have to get up in the middle of a charge to wait on customers!"

"Word of honor," Gage promised. "You're sure you want the French side?"

"The last time I fought for merry old England, I lost, remember?" She sat down across from him.

"Because your Saxons lacked discipline," he said. "But we are about three hundred and fifty years later now. The date is August twenty-sixth, 1346. Does that give you a clue?"

"Puts it somewhere in the middle of the Hundred Years' War, right?"

"Right. Know who this figure is?"

She frowned at the miniature he'd picked up. "An Edward?"

"Edward III. He's just invaded France. And this time the English army is paid, disciplined and professional, with a great respect for its archers. Your French army is still based on the feudal system, the nobility far more concerned with achieving individual glory on the battle-field than in using realistic strategy. And being quite feudal, they have no respect at all for their unmounted soldiers, who lack good training as well as any claim to decent breeding!"

"I get the feeling I may have picked the wrong side," Rani groaned suspiciously.

"You still outnumber me almost four to one," he pointed out encouragingly.

"What's the catch?" Rani regarded the board with a severe frown.

"This is the Battle of Crécy," he told her blandly.

"Crécy?" She glanced up, still frowning. "I've never set it up for Donna, but I seem to recall reading some-thing about it in one of her military history books . . ." Her voice trailed off thoughtfully as she tried to recall exactly what she had read.

"Don't worry about it, just fight it the way you think it should be fought," he advised easily.

"What do I get if I win?" she challenged lightly.

"I'll take you out to dinner," he returned at once. "And if I win, you can take me out."

Rani sobered. "Gage, when are you going to tell me your next argument for convincing me to go back to Dallas?"

"Over dinner. Now show me what the full flower of French chivalry can do against a paid professional army it outnumbers almost four to one."

From the beginning, Rani told herself, she was at a disadvantage. It was difficult to plot strategy while waiting on customers, and every time she did think of a particu-larly brilliant maneuver, Gage had a counter for it. He insisted the battle be fought according to the historical facts. The English bowmen, for example, got to loose their arrows with the aid of the sun behind them, shining in their enemies' eyes and glinting off the heavy French armor.

The French had to charge ponderously uphill, bearing the weight of their plate armor. The arrows glanced off the hardware, but the horses were not so well protected. If a knight had his animal shot out from under him, the odds were against his ever regaining his feet.

Gage fought in the manner typical of the English during the Hundred Years' War, remaining in a strong defensive position and leaving the charging and uphill struggling to the French.

"The amazing thing is that the French never seemed to learn," he observed at one point. "They kept making wild, reckless charges at the English, who decimated them with organized defense."

Rani winced. She had just thrown another contingent of gloriously attired armored knights into the fray.

"You've just ridden down several of your own infantry," Gage noted with interest. "Don't feel bad. It happened a lot in those days."

"All right! All right! I lose!" she finally exclaimed in exasperation shortly before lunch. "Another victory for disciplined professionalism." Her hand swept the remaining miniatures into a jumbled heap in the middle of the board. "Go get us some lunch. It's the least the victor can do!"

"You won't forget you owe me dinner?" he asked whimsically as he rose to his feet.

"I won't forget," she vowed ferociously. "I'll pick you up at seven."

He paused halfway to the door, looking mildly surprised. "You'll pick me up?"

"I'm the one taking you to dinner, right? I'll pick you up."

He looked vaguely pleased at the novelty. "You don't know where I live."

"Draw me a map!" she grumbled, getting up to wait on a customer who was about to enter the shop.

He nodded. "Interesting things, maps. You know they

didn't have them during the Middle Ages. At least not any reliable ones. Saved a lot of fighting."

Rani stared at him blankly, not understanding, but it was the customer who explained it to her with a grave nod toward Gage. "It was hard for the armies to find each other," the elderly stranger said. "They could wander around for months before coming into contact with the enemy."

"What an intelligent way to fight a war," Rani chuckled admiringly. Gage disappeared, gray eyes laughing at her.

In the afternoon business picked up and Rani was grateful. She wasn't in the mood to be invited to take part in another losing battle. But Gage spent the day manipulating the miniature warriors, and he turned out to be good for business. He fell into several long, highly technical conversations with the collectors of the small soldiers who ambled in. Rani wound up making several unexpected sales to the serious-faced men whose enthusiasm allowed them to get carried away with their hobby.

"Donna's going to be delighted, naturally," she remarked finally at closing time as she totaled out the register. "But don't you have a business of your own to run, Gage?"

"Right now you are my business," he reminded her, bringing home the realization that their own battle was about to recommence. And she couldn't avoid it; she had a map, she thought wryly.

With the proud, magnificently brave if not altogether intelligent attitude of one of her own French knights, Rani dressed for dinner that evening. Gage had left her off at her condominium right after work, telling her he would expect her promptly at seven. She didn't intend to be late.

Her wardrobe didn't run to the glamorous or the gaudy; it consisted mostly of jeans, tailored suits she had worn to work and a few evening outfits that would never come under the heading of sensational. But there was one interesting dress that Donna had helped her select during a visit to Dallas when the two sisters had gone on a shopping spree.

It was short and cut like a man's shirt, with a rakish collar and rolled back cuffs. But it was a deep black, very narrow and belted with a black patent-leather sash. For some reason the total effect, especially with several buttons undone at the collar, was raffish and piratical. Coupled with black high-heeled sandals and a loop of delicate silver chain around her exposed throat, it was chic and eye-catching. Donna had always had good taste in clothing.

She found Gage's home in a quiet upper-class neighborhood, which implied a certain amount of success in the business security field. The house was low, modern and surrounded by a walled courtyard. She parked her yellow Mazda in the drive and unhinged the wrought-iron gate.

To her surprise, the garden on the other side of the gate was not done in the familiar southwestern style, with brick fountains and lush greenery. The surroundings were rich and green, all right, and there was a fountain, but it was all done in a serenely tailored Japanese style. Rani walked slowly through the garden to the front door, coming to accept just how right the calm, restrained effect suited Gage Fletcher.

When he opened the door she found he was also wearing black, with only a crisp white shirt for contrast. The cut of the jacket was close-fitting and conservative. The sable of his hair gleamed faintly from the shower.

"We're going to make an entrance tonight, wherever we go," he mused appreciatively as his eyes roamed over her. "Are you sure you don't want to take the black Jag? Just for effect?"

"I'm sure," she laughed, feeling a rising excitement as she mentally prepared for the next battle maneuver from him.

"Want the psychological advantage of knowing you can beat a hasty retreat in your own war wagon?" he drawled understandingly.

"Perhaps," she admitted lightly as he stepped through the door. He didn't invite her in and Rani had only a glimpse of a hallway that seemed to carry on the Oriental motif. She found herself very interested in the interior of Gage's home. But then, she was freely acknowledging to herself now that she was very interested in Gage, period.

"I made reservations at a restaurant that features French food," she teased as they walked back through the garden. "I decided we'd better eat the loser's food. English cooking isn't exactly famous."

"Fine. Do you want me to drive?" he asked, absently holding out his hand for the keys.

"No, I do not! I'm taking you, remember?" She walked around to the driver's side of the Mazda and opened the door.

"Some aspects of male chauvinism die hard," he said apologetically as he slid in beside her.

"I'm aware of that," she pointed out somewhat caustically. "I worked for Aaron Prescott if you'll recall."

He nodded meekly. "I recall. Only too well. Are you going to make a pass at me after dinner when you bring me home?"

She flashed him a startled glance as she guided the Mazda out of the drive, and then her sense of humor rose to the fore. "Don't get your hopes up," she advised blandly. "Besides, you wouldn't want me to think you're unbecomingly aggressive or fast, would you?"

Gage didn't give her the next argument in his arsenal until they were halfway through the chicken Marengo, a dish named in honor of one of Napoleon's famous victories, as Gage took pains to point out.

"I've tried logic, which should have done the trick," he began, the humor in him fading as pure business took its place.

"You needn't waste any more time implying I'm not too bright," Rani countered grimly.

"Are you mercenary instead?" he shot back smoothly.

"What's that supposed to mean?" Suddenly tense, Rani put down her fork and waited.

"I've been authorized to offer you quite a sum of money, Rani," he stated calmly.

"Money! Good grief! How much?"

He told her and she swallowed in astonishment. "Prescott must be feeling quite desperate," she finally managed weakly.

"You could use that money to tide you over until you find another job," Gage pressed deliberately. "It would give you the financial cushion everyone needs while they look for work. You wouldn't have to rush into anything—"

"Tell Prescott to take his money and use it to spruce up the employees' cafeteria!" she flung back. "I sure as hell don't want it!"

"Rani," he began firmly, "be reasonable. You're going back to Dallas to clean up the mess you left behind. You might as well get paid for it!"

"I am not going back to Dallas, Gage. In fact, I am no more impressed by this argument than I was by the last one."

"You're being childish and vindictive, and the only one you're going to hurt is yourself! Can't you see that you're going to have to go back one way or another? Why do things the hard way?"

"Maybe I like doing them that way!"

"You're like the French during the Hundred Years' War: illogical, unreasonable and headed for a bruising fall! I will not allow it."

"You, Gage Fletcher, can't do anything about it! I'm sorry, but you're not going to earn your bounty fee off my hide!"

She had picked the only weapon she knew could sting him, and as usual it worked. She saw the anger wash chillingly into his gray eyes, watched the grooves at the edge of his mouth tauten. For a moment she thought he might do something violent, but in the next instant he had himself severely under control again.

Unhappily Rani wondered if the whole evening had just been ruined.

4

~~~~~~~~~~~~~~

When you look back over this evening and wonder what went wrong, you won't have far to search," Rani declared in exasperation as they walked back out to her car after the tension-filled meal. "You'll have only yourself to blame!"

Gage slid her a quelling glance, his features still set tightly. He hadn't lost his temper during the argument that had raged back and forth over the chicken Marengo, but he had steadily tried to erode her defenses, alternating between assaults of logic and outright bribery. Rani had stood firm against both, but she was beginning to realize she'd paid a steep price. It could have been such a lovely evening!

"For God's sake, Rani, you're too old for this kind of behavior!"

"Thanks!" she muttered dryly. "You do have a nice turn of phrase."

"Oh, hell, you know what I mean," he grumbled disgustedly as they reached her car.

"Ummm, yes, I believe I do. Nothing sadder than an aging female, is there? I'm certainly lucky King Tanner is willing to overlook my advancing years. There aren't many men who will even look at a woman after she turns thirty, you know," Rani informed him chattily as she slid behind the wheel. "Terrible discrimination against a woman after she turns thirty. I expect it will be even worse after I've reached forty."

"Will you stop going on about your age? I'm talking about your mental age, not your chronological one, and you know it!" Gage buckled his seat belt with such force that Rani realized he would much rather have been using his hands on her. "You're behaving like a willful teenager!"

"Reliving the lost days of my youth, no doubt." Rani guided the Mazda out into the street and headed back toward Gage's home. Was the man going to berate her all evening? It appeared so. Perhaps he had no more strings in his bow. The logic and the bribe hadn't worked. What else could he use?

Gage was silent for a long moment after her last jibe, staring sternly out the window. When he finally spoke again, his words surprised her. "Thank you for dinner."

"My pleasure," she retorted sarcastically. "The next time I take a man out, however, I think I'll make him sign a contract to the effect that he will be pleasant and sociable. As the one picking up the check, I think I have a right to expect at least some semblance of witty and charming conversation!"

There was a suspicious silence from the other side of the seat, and Rani threw a quick look in that direction. She discovered Gage's mouth curved upward in the first smile he had indulged in since the chicken Marengo.

"What's so funny?" she demanded.

"I was just thinking about what you said."

"Well, it's true! That meal cost me nearly sixty bucks with wine and tip. The least you could have been was pleasant!"

"Exactly how men have felt since time immemorial!" he shot back smoothly. "It's nice to get your money's worth out of a date!"

"Of all the male chauvinist remarks!" Rani gasped. But the outrage was tempered by her rising sense of humor, and in spite of herself she realized she was smiling.

Gage turned in his seat, one arm braced along the back of it, and studied her profile intently. "I'm sorry I ruined the evening for you," he finally said gently. "But you knew it was going to be partly business."

"*Partly!* More like one-hundred percent!"

"The night isn't over yet. And the business portion of the evening is finished as far as I'm concerned."

"Am I supposed to be grateful?" she challenged caustically.

"You're supposed to accept my invitation to come in and have a nightcap with me when we reach my place."

Rani's fingers tightened on the wheel. "Sorry, Gage. I don't switch gears that fast. The evening's gone sour and that's that."

"You're wrong," he told her with quiet emphasis. "The portion of the evening that took place on the battlefield has come to an inconclusive ending, I'll grant you, but what happens next is off the battlefield, remember?"

"Trust a man to think the two arenas can be separated!"

"You gave me your word, Rani. Whatever happens between the two of us on a personal level has nothing to do with the business side of things."

"Having failed to achieve your main goal this evening, you're now going to try for your secondary one?" Rani turned the car into his drive, fully intending to let Gage out and be on her way. She was annoyed with him for having made a battle out of dinner, and she was even more irritated to learn he now expected to seduce her!

He reached out with a sudden, swift movement and removed the keys from the ignition as she switched off the engine, pocketing them before she could do more than exclaim angrily. "Come in and have a drink, Rani. Please."

"Give me back those keys!"

"I'm not going to let you drive off in this mood. There are things I want to say to you—"

"You can't stop me! Now give me back those keys!" She held out her palm imperiously, not at all certain she could outbluff him but knowing she had to try.

"Are you going to turn this side of things into a battle, too?" he asked with exasperation. His eyes gleamed at her in the darkness, and there was a tension in the way he sprawled in his seat. A tension that signaled danger.

"And if I am?" she dared, rising recklessly to his challenge.

"If you are, then you'd better be prepared to take the consequences. This is one battle I can win tonight!"

"Don't be so damn sure of yourself!" Her voice was husky with the depths of a provocative defiance she couldn't quite explain, even to herself. It had something to do with the fact that she didn't want the evening to end with bitterness between them—didn't want it to end that way but was unable to gracefully make the transition he wanted from her. She was caught in a trap from which she wasn't sure how to extricate herself.

Gage uncoiled with the speed of a pouncing cat, clasping her shoulders in two strong hands before she realized his intention. "It's not that I'm so damn sure of myself," he growled, hauling her toward him until she collapsed against his chest in a helpless tangle of arms and legs. "It's just that I'm so damn *desperate!*"

Cradling her forcibly against him as he leaned back into the confining corner between seat and door, Gage anchored her head with fingers laced into the loose knot of her hair. "I've been looking forward to *this* part of the evening all afternoon. You're not going to ruin things for me now!"

Rani tried to frame a protest, but before she could do so her mouth was suddenly captive to his and a surging excitement roared through her veins. Gage seemed intent on stamping his seal of possession on her lips, not requiring a response yet, merely surrender. Merely! Rani was instantly dazed at the impact of his kiss.

It burned into her senses as he slowly, deliberately, deepened the heated, damp contact. His mouth slid firmly across hers, softening it, quelling the signs of defiance, forcing an obedient retreat. That goal accomplished, he began to probe into the territory beyond, urging her lips apart with a thrusting strength that literally took away Rani's breath.

"Oh!" The moan was uttered deep in her throat, but he heard it and read it for what it was, an admission of growing response that she could not contain.

Her fingertips moved like small daggers, moving over the black jacket that enveloped his shoulders and up into the midnight of his hair. She heard his groan of mounting passion and felt his body hardening under hers.

"My God, woman! Can you feel what you're doing to me?" he breathed into her mouth.

"I didn't start this," she tried to say, but he ignored her words.

"Yes, you did, and what's more, you're going to finish it." He took his hand away from her disarrayed hair and fumbled for the door handle. "But I'm not going to let you finish it here. At our advanced age we deserve a little comfort."

She sensed the humor in him and wasn't sure if she wanted to succumb to it. Doing so would only be that much more of a surrender. But it was hard to resist. The warm night air was waiting to enfold them as the door swung open and Gage began easing himself out from under her light weight. "Come inside, Rani, and I'll show you how pleasant a date I can be when I try," he coaxed a little thickly as he caught her wrist and began pulling her out of the seat.

"You're very arrogant tonight," she whispered, holding back as she tried to make up her mind.

"Am I? I expect it's because that's the only option you've left me. I get the feeling that if I don't take charge, you're going to let your own silly arrogance push you into driving away tonight without a backward glance. Just remember you're the one who decided to make a battle out of what should have been a very pleasant night for both of us!"

Rani clutched at the frame of the car door, refusing to be pulled free. Her eyes glittered with challenge as she looked up at him. "I don't think I'm going to let you manhandle me into this," she drawled firmly. "It would be a sign of weakness on my part, and you would undoubtedly read far too much into it!"

"A sign of weakness!" he rasped, swinging back to confront her. "Is that what you call sheer obstinate, stubborn, illogical feminine contrariness? I'll show you a sign of weakness!"

He moved close, and Rani resisted the urge to slide backward along the seat, knowing he would only pursue. Boldly she eyed him, her legs curled under her as she sat waiting tensely. "I don't know what you think you're going to do, Gage, but if—"

"You're intent on provoking me this evening, aren't you? Well, wait until you see what that gets you!" His hand flashed out and in a moment he had captured both her wrists, manacling them together. Then he used the grip to pull her swiftly, lightly, from the car until she was standing in front of him.

"Gage!" A little shocked at the unexpected roughness of the treatment, Rani was even more startled when he swooped and lifted her high into his arms.

"*This* is a sign of weakness!" he informed her brusquely, striding for the gate. "When a man has to go to these lengths to get himself ravished after a dinner date, *weak* is about all you can call him, isn't it?"

"Gage, put me down, you idiot!" Rani was torn between laughter and outrage. And underlying both emotions was the pulsing throb of a rising intoxication. "If you're trying to come across as the injured party, you're not doing very well! This is hardly a sign of weakness!"

"Ah, but it is." He looked down at her in the moonlight as he pushed open the gate into the Japanese-style garden. "I'm weak with longing for you, my sweet battle maid. Haven't you realized that yet?"

Rani stared up at him, wide-eyed with wonder not untinged by a trickle of fear as she sensed the passion flowing like an electrical current between them. She knew as the iron gate clanged shut behind them that she wasn't going to have much chance resisting this man tonight.

But what he was offering was so dangerous, she reminded herself swiftly. It was an elemental, threatening emotion that she had always told herself she didn't want, couldn't risk. Yet, the hunger in her had been ignited the night before, during the embrace by the whirlpool, and hunger was a hard drive to deny. It made one take risks, dare fate, break self-made rules, she was discovering.

Gage must have sensed some sign of impending surrender to whatever the evening still held for both of them. When he set her on her feet in the serene foyer, his gaze was smoky. "The spoils of war," he muttered huskily as he bent his head to brush a light, tantalizing little kiss against her nose.

Rani shivered and found herself stepping back a pace. Her awareness of him was making her feel nervous and tense. "Under the circumstances that's not the most diplomatic thing you could have said."

He arched one brow in mocking interest. "No? But then, I didn't say which of us I considered as the spoils, did I? Come into my parlor, little fly, and have a glass of cognac. Now that you're this far, I'm willing to declare a truce."

With one hand planted at the small of her back he guided her through the living room with its tranquil and sophisticated Oriental-inspired design. The furniture was low and modern and quietly masculine. Low ebony tables and chairs were upholstered in austere, exotic patterns. A pair of Asian bronze lions guarded the fireplace, and a beautifully painted coromandel screen stood in one corner. There was a set of antique swords mounted over the low couch, and the bookcases along one wall were filled with books on military history. The floor-to-ceiling windows opened on the garden, which was softly illuminated. The room was rather like its master, Rani thought: restrained, fascinating and not easily classified.

He seated her amid the dark cushions of the couch and went to a teak cabinet to pour cognac into snifters. She watched him, trying to read the nuances of his movements, sense the direction of his thoughts. Her own simmering excitement was tinged with a strange ambivalence, and for a moment, as he poured the cognac, she attempted to analyze it.

The yearning in her was a tangible force, but it was tempered with the restraints imposed by years of caution and self-protection. It was as if this man might somehow be asking too much of her too soon. Rani wanted time to understand this new element in her life. There was no denying the power of the emotions rippling between them, but that very factor made her tense and wary. She had told herself for so long that she wanted serenity and calm in a relationship, yet here she was becoming involved in one that was just the opposite. She needed time.

There was so much they did not yet know about each other, Rani reminded herself. Much still stood between them. It would be wiser not to allow the seduction of the night to influence her.

He turned away from the teak cabinet, a balloon glass in each hand, and across the room their eyes collided and locked. He thinks he has me, Rani realized abruptly, swallowing a wave of nervousness that sprang to life from nowhere. He thinks all he has to do now is reach out and take my hand and lead me off to bed. Was that the way it was? Was that the way she wanted it?

Without a word he closed the distance between them, handing her one of the glasses. But instead of sitting down beside her, he remained standing, sipping from the cognac snifter in a small salute, his eyes poring over her intently. Then he swung around and paced to the window and stood for a long moment staring out into the shadowy garden. The tension began to heighten in Rani's body as she waited for the next move.

This was ridiculous! She was a thirty-two-year-old woman who was fully capable of diplomatically guiding such man-woman scenes. What was the matter with her tonight? Why was she allowing this man to shake her composure? If she didn't want the drama to go any further, all she had to do was rise, excuse herself politely and drive home! Yet, there she sat, like a captive Sabine waiting for her new master to enjoy her at his leisure. Rani took another sip of the aromatic cognac, mentally stiffening her resolve. Yes, she was going to have to get control of this situation while she could still do so.

But before she could find the words to gently but firmly bring a close to the evening, Gage spoke quietly, his broad back still to her as he gazed into the garden.

"There's something we should have out in the open, Rani."

Startled, her eyes narrowed slightly as she stared at the dark mass of his body. "More arguments on behalf of Prescott Services?" she tried to ask lightly.

The hand holding his snifter shifted in a small, impatient movement. "This has nothing to do with Prescott— only you and me." She could have sworn he drew a determined breath before going on. "If you stay with me tonight, Rani, everything changes," he finally announced evenly.

The glass in Rani's fingers trembled a little at the intensity of his words. "I don't quite understand, Gage."

He turned slowly to look at her, and the very carefulness of the movement put her on edge as nothing else could have done. It emphasized clearly how serious he was when he went on to explain his meaning.

"I want you," he began, each word a link in a chain he was forging; a chain with which he meant to bind her. "I've been wanting you since I first saw you preparing to fight the Battle of Hastings. When I kissed you last night, I knew you wanted me, too, at least a little. I've already told you that whatever happens between us has nothing to do with Prescott Services, Incorporated. But what I haven't told you is that I'm not interested in a one-night stand."

Rani lowered her lashes to conceal the wariness in her tawny eyes. "That's always reassuring to hear, of course."

"I'm glad you find it so," he replied immediately. "But I wonder if you realize exactly what I'm trying to say. Rani, if you stay tonight, you'll belong to me by morning. There will be no going back to Tanner or Brady or any other man who catches your eye. I'm a possessive man, and it would be foolish and perhaps dangerous for either of us to pretend otherwise. If you stay with me tonight, you will be starting an affair, a full-fledged affair, not a one-night stand. Do you understand what I'm trying to say? I won't share you with any other man. For as long as our arrangement lasts, you will be totally faithful. You will not treat it as a casual fling!"

Rani caught her breath. "I didn't think you believed in *love* affairs, Gage."

His eyes grew smokier. "This has nothing to do with love. This has to do with a whole lot of much more basic and realistic emotions. Possessiveness and sheer male pride, for starters. I want a woman I can trust, one I know belongs to me."

"And when the *arrangement* ends?" she whispered tautly, a flicker of fear sizzling through her veins.

He hesitated a fraction too long, and Rani realized he

hadn't really thought about it. He'd probably been too busy worrying about how to tell her he expected complete fidelity! "When it ends it will be by mutual agreement—everything honest and aboveboard. There will be no sneaking around behind each other's back, trying to line up a new partner before taking the step of ending our relationship. But I see no reason why our arrangement shouldn't last for a long time, Rani," he added. "I think you and I are rather well suited."

"That's a rather sweeping judgment to make, isn't it? Given the fact that we've only known each other a short time and still have a somewhat unresolved matter of business between us?" She didn't know why she felt the urge to provoke him that night. Perhaps it was the arrogance of his words, coupled with the way he assumed he could move back and forth between the business and the personal aspects of their relationship. Personally she didn't find the shuttle so easy. Nor did she care for the high-handed way he was setting down rules. Gage Fletcher was assuming the role of the victorious general a bit too quickly for her liking. He needed to learn that his opponent wasn't equally content to play the part of defeated victim. Spoils of war indeed!

He surveyed her as she sat on his couch, her slender body curled there with a kind of cool tension. "The judgment may be sweeping, but I'd stake my honor on the accuracy of it. I'm sure we're well suited, Rani. What I'm not sure of is that you realize it yet. You're still confusing the business and personal angles. Forget the Prescott Services side of this tonight. Concentrate on the two of us," he urged gently.

"Even if I do that, I find I still have some reservations," she murmured dryly, lifting her glass to her lips. "You're asking for a great deal on such short acquaintance, Gage. I'm not at all sure I'm ready to make the sort of commitment you're requiring for the sake of your masculine ego."

She saw the tendons in his wrist tighten as he gripped

the stem of his glass. Was he growing annoyed with her? Her own recklessness grew at the thought. "Do you want only a one-night fling, then, Rani?" he challenged.

At once she shook her head, mouth curving in wry amusement. "No. I'm no more interested in that kind of thing than you seem to be."

"Then there's really no alternative, is there?" he pounced. "By staying tonight, you'll be committing yourself to an affair with me. If you don't want the one, you must want the other."

She shook her head once in denial. "You seem to be forgetting that there's a third alternative."

"What's that?"

"I don't have to stay tonight. Very simple." Resolutely she rose to her feet, gracefully depositing the empty snifter on the low table in front of the couch. Straightening, her gaze clashed abruptly with his and she knew a shiver of apprehension. "I'm not nearly as sure of what I want yet as you seem to be, Gage. You're trying to push me tonight, and I don't think I want to be pushed. The best answer is to provide myself with a little more time. I'm going home. Alone. I hope you enjoyed the evening." Her decision made at last, Rani gave him her most brilliant smile and made for the door.

"No!" She hadn't gotten five steps before he was on her, reaching out to snag her wrist and jolt her to a stop. "Rani, you're not going anywhere tonight. Stop playing games with me, woman!"

His eyes blazed down at her, and the hard line of his mouth was set in grim resolve. It was becoming increasingly difficult to defy him, she realized uneasily. And a part of her seemed to be thriving on having elicited this dangerous response in him. What was the matter with her? He was right. She was too old to be playing games like this. On the other hand, she'd never had the desire or the opportunity to play them before. They seemed somehow a part of the reckless passion he created in her.

But I'm not playing games, she told herself in the next

breath, and then she repeated it aloud for his benefit.
"I'm not playing games, Gage. I mean it. I think both of
us need more time. Everything's happening too fast and I
won't be pushed into this . . . this *arrangement* you
seem to want."

"It's too late. You're already involved in it," he grated
softly, fingers tightening around the small bones of her
wrist as he drew her inexorably close. "I didn't go to the
effort of carrying you in here tonight just to watch you
walk back out the door!"

He set his glass down absently and lifted his hand to
touch the taut line of her throat. Rani trembled as his
excitingly rough fingertip traced a path down to the point
where the collar of her black dress opened. Instinctively
she tried to step back, but the tip of his probing finger
never lost contact with her skin.

"Gage, we both know you won't force yourself on
me," she whispered.

"Do we?"

"Now you're the one who's playing games. Arrogant
male games. And I don't like them."

His head moved once in a crisp negative response.
"Why are you fighting me? You want this as much as I
do."

"I'm not sure yet what I want," she protested.

"Then I'll help you make up your mind!" He dragged
her against his chest, his hands sliding upward to spear
into her hair and hold her head still for his kiss. Rani
opened her mouth in a small exclamation of refusal, but
the words were lost in the depths of his throat as he
sealed her lips with his own.

She felt the willpower in him as the purely masculine
urge to dominate lapped at her, seeking to innundate her
senses. She'd aroused something else in him besides
desire, something that bordered on the dangerous. For
the first time in her life the knowledge that she was
ultimately in control began to slip from her grasp. She

began to perceive where her strange recklessness had led her that night, and she wasn't able to analyze her own emotions far enough to decide whether or not to resist.

Gage held her forcefully but without hurting her, his mouth feeding on the honeyed depths behind her lips. His tongue surged inward, circling the delicate skin just inside her mouth and then probing the barrier of her teeth.

In a small gesture of defiance she nipped at the invading force of his tongue and was instantly punished when he withdrew it to close his teeth warningly on her lower lip.

"Oh!" Her gasp was a combination of pain that wasn't quite pain and anger that wasn't quite anger. What was the matter with her? She clutched at his shoulders, her nails sinking into the fabric of his jacket as he once again took control of her mouth. When she shivered in his grasp, he groaned in husky satisfaction, and then his hands slid heavily down to the curve of her shoulders, kneading the skin just inside the rakish collar.

"Rani, Rani," he grated thickly against her mouth. "Did you really think I would let you walk out that door tonight?"

"You have to give me the option." she tried to say, only to have him lift one hand to silence her.

"No, I don't have to give you the option." Her eyes flared with gold as she challenged him mutely over the edge of his silencing palm. "Where did you get the idea that I feel obliged to fight fair?" he went on meaningfully. "I know you want me, honey. Probably not anywhere near as much as I want you, but I'm willing to work on that!"

"You assume far too much," she muttered tightly as he lowered his hand. "You're arrogant and domineering, and I can't afford to let you ride roughshod over me!"

"And you're stubborn and willful and unbelievably provoking. But I *am* going to ride you tonight. You're very brave on the field of battle, sweetheart, but you're not going to win this skirmish. I swear that before morning comes you'll belong to me, and I promise not to leave you with the impression that my riding is rough-shod!"

"You're too damn sure of yourself!" she gasped heatedly.

"No," he confessed, surprising her. His mouth twisted wryly. "It's just that I want you so much, I can't do anything else except set the seal on our relationship. If I don't, you'll continue to goad me and tease me. . . ."

"That's not true! I'm not a tease!"

"Only because I'm not going to allow you to play that part!" he shot back unevenly. Then, holding her pinned to his side with one hand, he deliberately began undoing the buttons of the black shirt dress. His eyes burned into her. Rani felt strangely helpless to halt the progress of his hand. This was what she wanted, deep down inside. She longed to know the feel of him on her skin, longed to wrap him close and take him into her. The lure of passion had never been this strong, swamping her common sense and making her shiver so beneath a man's touch.

Gage finished unbuttoning the bodice of the dress but made no effort to push aside the edges of the material. Instead he left her breasts in their shadowy concealment and sought the black patent-leather sash.

"Wait," Rani said with a last spark of urgency, trying to halt his fingers as he pried loose the black sash. "I want to talk this out, Gage. We must come to an understanding . . . !" If only she could instill some sense of rational calm into the situation!

"We will by morning," he assured her huskily as the sash came free.

"No, now. Tonight. Before this has gone too far!"

"It's already gone much too far for you to retreat, honey," he told her, draping the black leather sash over his shoulder before shoving his hands up into the opening of the loosened dress. When she opened her mouth to protest again, he kissed her. Automatically her hands went to his shoulders, and under the impact of his lips she went limp.

He used the moment of weakness to push the dress off completely, pulling it down her arms and over her hips until it fell into a foam of darkness at her feet. It left her naked from the waist up, and Rani's first half-hysterical thought was that she should have worn a bra. It would have been at least one more barrier—would have bought her a little more time. Now only a wispy triangle of black satin shielded her from the smoking eyes. Somehow even her shoes had come off.

The shock of finding herself so suddenly naked brought another gilding of angry gold into her gaze as she faced him challengingly. "I won't let you manhandle me, damn it!"

"You can't stop me. Not tonight." His hands went to her waist, finding the curve of it with blatant pleasure as he took in the sight of her high, firm breasts. Slowly he began to draw her close once more, and even though her blood was racing through her veins now, Rani made one last attempt to regain control of the situation.

"Let me go, Gage!" She moved abruptly, pushing at his chest in an effort to break his grip on her waist. "I'm not a captive of war who happens to be available for your amusement!"

For an instant she thought she had actually succeeded in freeing herself and didn't know whether to be elated or disappointed. His fingers fell away from her bare waist, but an instant later he had used his hands to trap her wrists. Holding them with one gentle fist, he reached up to his shoulder for the black leather sash.

"Gage!" Stunned, she uttered his name in a shocked gasp as he deftly knotted the sash around her wrists, chaining her. Her eyes flew down to the soft leather binding and then lifted incredulously to his unyielding face. She saw the flaring desire there and knew the echo of it in herself. The dazzling physical tension was making her weak in a way she had never before experienced.

"Don't look so shocked, honey," he drawled deeply, taking hold of the trailing end of the leather sash. "You're a prize I would have been more than happy to carry off any battlefield in any era."

With unmistakable purposefulness he moved, lifting her high into his arms and gliding across the living room with the stride of a conqueror.

5

Rani's immediate reaction to being literally carried off to bed was a mixture of outrage, passion and a strange sense of inevitability. She caught sight of herself in the full-length bronze-tinted mirrors that lined one wall of the corridor, and her sense of shock deepened.

The vision of herself naked and bound, her hair in tumbling disarray around her shoulders, was mind-stunning. The outrage surfaced. "Gage, stop this! How dare you treat me like this? I swear to God, I'll . . . Oh!"

The last exclamation was a gasp of dismay as he turned the corner into a shadowed room. The thick carpet under her feet as he set her down was a sleek, dark gray. The ebony-framed bed was covered with a black quilt and the tables on either side were beautifully worked with an exotic inlay. Two restrained, subtly sensuous paintings done in the Japanese style framed the bed. It was a dark and exotic room, and Rani felt its effects immediately.

"Enough, Rani," Gage growled richly as he held her in front of him. "You know damn well I'm not going to stop now, and if you're honest you'll admit you don't want me to!"

"If you go through with this . . ." she threatened shakily as he continued to hold the end of the leather sash in one hand while lifting his free one to her throat.

"If . . . ?" he challenged coolly.

She flushed, aware that the color started as low as her breasts and rose upward. He stared down at the telltale wave of pink as though fascinated, and then he touched the tip of one nipple as if it were a valuable gem. Rani drew in her breath, her whole body tightening in reaction. "There's no *if* about it, honey."

Somehow, Rani thought wildly, this shouldn't be happening. Not to her! This wasn't the kind of man or the kind of passion she sought or needed. What was wrong with her tonight that she had become enmeshed in something so dangerous? Why did she feel this wild singing in her bloodstream or this throbbing sensation deep in her stomach? And as for Gage! Dear God! Gage had no right to look at her as if he intended to own her.

All these thoughts whirled in her head, and then Gage bent to kiss her. Rani stopped thinking coherently at all.

He placed her bound hands against his chest and lowered them deliberately to the buttons of his shirt. Fingers trembling, her eyes heavy with passion at the reality of what was happening, Rani obediently began to undo the fastenings of the white garment. As she worked slowly, awkwardly, Gage released her to shrug out of the black jacket. His mouth didn't leave hers until the shirt had followed the jacket onto the floor and he stood before her wearing only the dark slacks.

Rani found herself unable to resist trailing her bound hands across the hardness of his bronzed chest. In deepening wonder she brushed her nails lightly across the flat nipples, and Gage whispered her name into her hair. Then he whispered something else, a phrase of such bluntly erotic passion that she trembled as if at a caress.

"Heaven help you, Gage Fletcher, if you turn out to be the kind of man who is arrogant in victory!" she warned on a sigh of surrender. She leaned into him, running her fingers down through the crisply curling black hair that disappeared under the waistband of his slacks. "One gloating word tomorrow morning and I'll have your head on a silver platter!" She couldn't bear it if he gloated later.

Gage groaned, a combination of rueful amusement and rising need. "I promise that you won't regret tonight, sweetheart. We're going to be so good together, you and I."

She could not fight him any longer and they both knew it. Her head spinning, Rani let herself be drawn into the waiting pool of passion and excitement, closing off all thought of the past and the future. For tonight this man would be her entire world. She did not understand how it could have happened this way, with a man who was so different from what she had always thought she wanted, but she could no longer argue with reality.

In a haze of mounting sensation she let her hands explore the contours of his chest once again until they found their path blocked by the belt of his slacks. Gage's eyes burned into hers, his callous fingertips circling her hardening nipples as she fumbled with the buckle of his belt. A moment later he wore only the masculine version of her one remaining garment, a pair of white undershorts that already revealed the evidence of his desire.

"Sweetheart!" On a muttered sigh, Gage's hands slid down her soft belly and around to her derriere, cupping the curves and drawing her abruptly close to his thighs.

Unable to do anything else, Rani lifted her arms and encircled his neck as he forced her into the straining, heated cradle of his hips. She felt his hands clench luxuriously into the fullness of the rounded globes of her bottom, and then she was made startlingly aware of the waiting power in him. He wanted her to know of it, she realized vaguely—wanted her to know and accept the male challenge of him.

"Gage, oh, Gage . . ."

His name was a whisper of sound on her lips, and as if he could not resist the plea, Gage stopped briefly to lift her into his arms. Rani's senses swam and she closed her eyes, not opening them again until she felt the thick black quilt beneath her. As her lashes lifted slightly she looked up through them at the man who stood gazing down at her.

He was excitingly beautiful to her senses, overwhelmingly male, uncompromisingly aroused. Rani's pulse throbbed and the blood in her veins turned molten. She had a sudden atavistic urge to flee from the rush of desire and knew in the same moment that flight was impossible.

But the impulse existed. He was massive, too strong, too overpoweringly male in a way she couldn't have described but that the feminine core of her knew and understood completely. When he moved, the soft light gleaming on his flanks and shoulders, she edged instinctively away, rolling onto her side and attempting to slip off the bed.

"Rani!" Gage's voice cracked with strange urgency. "Don't run from me. It's too late. . . ."

She felt the bed give beneath his weight as he came down on it with one knee. A second later a large hand closed over her shoulder, spinning her back down beneath him.

For a timeless moment she stared up at him with the primitive uncertainty of a woman who knows herself caught and bound by a man. He knelt over her, his hands pinning her shoulders, his eyes glittering with his own very masculine certainty. But there was a gentleness in his touch that was suddenly reassuring, and there was a waiting look in him, as if he would go no further until she knew and understood what was happening. Slowly, he caught her hands and unlaced the leather sash.

And very abruptly, everything was all right. Rani stopped fighting him and reached up to pull his head down to hers. This was what she wanted and needed. How could she have thought of running from him?

"No, no, my darling," she breathed. "I won't run. Not from you. Not tonight. Put your hands on me, Gage. Touch me, hold me."

"Rani!" He groaned the name once more against her mouth before consuming the passion behind her lips. Strong fingers moved across her breasts, seeking the tight, aching peaks. When she arched upward into his hand, he muttered fiercely sensuous words that were as fiery as his touch. Rani shivered beneath them and tried to pull him closer.

She was on fire now, willing to do anything he asked of her, eager to please and be pleased. His palms grazed the softness of her breasts and she cried out with the sweet agony of her need.

At last he ducked his sable head out from under the chain of her arms and found her nipples with his mouth. As she reacted, straining against him, he moved the flat of his hand down to her stomach, stripping off the black satin panties.

"Please, Gage, please . . . !"

"Do you want me, sweetheart?"

"My God! You must *know!*" She lifted her hips against his hand as he traced a tantalizing path downward.

He circled her nipple with his tongue one last time and then began dropping hot, stinging little kisses across the satin skin of her stomach as his fingers feathered the swell of her thighs.

Rani's nails clung, digging deeply into one broad shoulder as she turned and twisted beneath his touch. Her eyes were squeezed shut and her toes curled into the heavy dark quilt.

When at last his hand teased closer to the apex of her legs, Rani thought she would go out of her head with the force of aching desire. She waited breathlessly for him to gently part her thighs, and when he didn't she whispered his name over and over again in sensual, feminine demand.

"Show me," he taunted passionately, lightly toying with the triangle of hair hiding the ultimate goal. "Show me how much you want me. Open yourself to me; invite me inside. I need to know I'm wanted."

Slowly, with the most indescribably wanton sensation, Rani obeyed the command. Her legs parted for him and she felt his sudden indrawn breath as he gently probed the secret recesses of her. Rani was astounded at how incredibly vulnerable it made her feel to find herself responding to his passionate demand. When he touched her in that most intimate of places, she moaned his name and sank her teeth delicately into his shoulder.

"You're on fire, honey," he rasped thickly as his fingers found the flowing warmth of her. "On fire for *me!*"

"Yes!" How could she deny it? "Gage, I want you. I can't believe how much I need you!"

"Not half as much as I need you!" He moved, propelled by a desire that could no longer be denied. Lifting her wrists high over her head so that her breasts were drawn high and taut, he settled himself firmly between her legs.

Rani caught her breath sharply as she felt the first tentative, testing thrust into her softness. Gage hesitated a moment longer as if wanting to absorb the sight of her at the instant of claiming. She tried to free her arms so that she could wrap him close, but he continued to pin them above her head, gazing down into her passion-softened face with eyes that held the heat of burning coals.

"My God, Rani! My God . . . !" And then he was surging into her, shocking her body with the force of his sensual impact.

"Oh!" For an instant she couldn't even breathe as she

tried to adjust to the overwhelming presence within her. He let his full weight sprawl along the length of her slenderness, crushing her deep into the quilt. She felt taken, chained, claimed, and her only defense was to claim him in turn.

She arched upward in reaction to the driving thrust of his hips, twisting her head to nip savagely at the contour of his shoulder, curving her body into his.

Gage responded in kind, meeting her with the full power of his manhood. His teeth closed with excruciating gentleness, first around the tips of her breasts and then around the tips of her earlobes. With one hand he continued to hold her wrists above her head, and with the other he reached down to catch her hips, forcing her to meet the rhythm he was establishing.

Their bodies surged together as the ultimate goal neared for both. Neither spared the other and neither wanted to be spared. The sheen of perspiration that coated their limbs gave evidence of the intense energy flaring between them.

When at last Rani felt herself slipping beyond control, she called Gage's name once more and then went momentarily rigid beneath him.

"Yes, Rani, *yes!*" he urged thickly, burying his face in her tangled hair as the small ripples began to wash over her body. "Sweetheart . . ." And then he was joining her in the final ecstasy, his own body forging deeply into her, reveling in the rapturous victory that belonged to both of them.

Gage emerged from the aftermath of the lovemaking with a sense of satisfaction that went beyond anything he had ever known. He raised his head to look down into her face, captivated by the soft way her lashes feathered her cheek as she lay quietly beneath him.

Soft. Everything about her, once a man got past the sharp barricades of her independence, was soft. He stared at her wonderingly, aware of a fierce pleasure. His intuition had been right. She was far more vulnerable than she realized, he thought, and with that realization came the knowledge that he must protect her from the results of her own brave pride and determination. She needed his protection, and now he had made her his responsibility in the most fundamental way. This unbelievably soft and passionate woman had given herself to him, whether she fully realized it or not, and he would see to it that she was kept safe. His mouth curved a little in wry acknowledgment of the fact that his desire to protect her was not particularly altruistic. He sure as hell did not want any other man taking on the responsibility! She was his.

The impact of his decision made him catch his breath. Never had he felt such a sense of certainty about the future. He knew beyond a shadow of a doubt that he would not be able to let Rani go even if she were to run from him. He would have no choice but to follow and bring her back. She needed him to look after her. She needed him to guard the softness. And right now the only way to protect her was to take her back to Dallas. He would not allow the threat of Aaron Prescott to hang over her like a sword of Damocles.

Rani opened her eyes to find Gage staring down at her, and the hard determination she saw in his face made her suddenly, vividly, aware of what had just happened. She had recklessly thrown herself into a passionate encounter with a man who seemed the totally opposite of the kind of man she had always thought she wanted. How could she let a man goad her into battle and then into bed?

At that thought a warm red stained her cheeks and she lowered her lashes once again, unable to meet the intense gaze above her.

"You sure as hell won't need to wonder if I'm faithful," Gage murmured on a note of contented masculine humor. "Dealing with you in my bed won't leave me any energy for handling other women!"

Rani flicked him an appraising glance from behind the concealment of her lashes. "Are you trying to tell me something, Gage?"

"I'm only reaffirming what I said earlier." He leaned over a couple of inches to plant a light kiss on her forehead. "We're together now, you and I. There will be no one else for either of us."

He was claiming her for an affair. Rani tried to sort through her muddled reactions to that information and found herself bogged down in quicksand. She honestly wasn't sure what her feelings were at that moment. They almost defied description. A part of her still resented the way he was driving her into an arrangement, but another part of her felt helpless to resist. How could she have been so thoroughly seduced by a man who was neither comfortable nor serene?

"Remember what I said about arrogant victors," she tried to drawl lightly in an effort to meet the masculine satisfaction in him with something approaching nonchalance. But the words came out all wrong. They came out sounding fearful and defensive.

He didn't seem to notice. "Are you admitting I'm the victor tonight?"

"Of course not!"

"Oh, well. I've still got a few more hours to try wringing the admission out of you," he decided philosophically.

"Not a chance," she asserted.

"If I can't manage it here in bed, my coffee will probably do the trick in the morning," he warned, and lowered himself to her once more.

Rani awoke the next morning with a temporary sensation of complete disorientation. She was not accustomed to waking up in beds other than her own, she thought wryly, glancing around the austerely elegant room. Doing so was unsettling. She really was set in her ways. In a strange house one didn't just hop out of bed and traipse down the hall to plug in the coffee. On top of that, one had to spend time wondering where the bathroom was. And then there was the awkwardness of not having a closet full of fresh clothing from which to choose.

All her normal routines were going to be short-circuited that morning. I've become a creature of habit, she thought, sitting slowly up in bed as her gaze fell on the magnificent masculine body next to her. This man, she acknowledged, was going to be the cause of her learning some new habits. An affair with Gage Fletcher.

She rolled the words around in her mind, drinking in the expanse of his tanned back, which was exposed above the white sheet that was gathered at his lean waist. An affair with Gage Fletcher. The very thought sent a shiver of uneasy excitement through her, and the memory of the previous night's passion reinforced that tremor.

How long would he want the arrangement to last?

That question was enough to send her sliding toward the edge of the bed. Standing up, her toes buried in the thick pile of the gray rug, Rani was suddenly conscious of a delicious ache in the muscles of her inner thighs. It was not all that different from the ache she had experienced after the horseback-riding session on King's ranch. Grimacing, Rani reminded herself that the night before it was Gage who had done the riding. Not at all sure she liked that image, she began a determined hunt for the bath.

It wasn't hard to find. Stepping inside and closing the door quietly behind her, she surveyed the impressive scene. The huge tub and the other porcelain fixtures were all done in a deep shade of red, and the room was mirrored completely on two walls. The tub was reached via a couple of tiled steps, so that when standing within it one had a tranquil view of an enclosed garden just beyond the glass wall. The room was tiled in a material that looked like lustrous gray granite. The towels were as red as the fixtures. Whoever had decorated Gage's home had definitely had an eye for effect. But somehow the decor suited the man who lived in it. Quiet, dark, menacing.

An affair with Gage Fletcher. With deep curiosity Rani poked and probed among the items of masculine paraphernalia sitting on the red marble countertop. How long would it last?

Until he had convinced her to go back to Prescott Services long enough to straighten out the mess she had left behind?

Rani froze as the possible answer leaped into her mind. Across the room she watched her slender figure in the wall of mirrors, seeing the uneasy, uncertain expression on her own face. But he wanted her, she told the image silently. After last night there could be no doubt of it. And she wanted to believe him when he said the arrangement between them was separate from the battle they were fighting.

Thrusting aside the questions and the potentially disturbing answers, Rani stepped toward the tub, peering down at the brass fixtures. She got the temperature of the water adjusted and pulled the red shower curtain behind her as she stepped inside. It was strange showering while looking out into a garden. It was as if she were outdoors. Laughing silently at her own fancy, Rani gave herself up to the pulsing water.

Lost in a bemused state somewhere between rational thought and erotic memory, Rani was jolted back to full awareness only when the red curtain was tugged aside sometime later and Gage stepped in beside her. He grinned lazily down into her upturned face and kissed the tip of her nose.

"Good morning, Lady Knight," he began with a grand flourish. "Or should that be lady of the night?" he amended thoughtfully. "Ouch!" Reaching down to massage his shin where she had lightly kicked him, Gage stared up at her with a distinctly hurt expression.

"I don't care for jokes, bad or otherwise, at this hour of the morning," she advised sweetly, grabbing a red washcloth and lathering it up hurriedly.

"I'll try to remember that," he muttered, straightening. But his eyes gleamed as he eyed her. "Actually, I'm not accustomed to making jokes at this hour of the day. Which probably explains why it didn't come off too well. Here, let me do that." He removed the washcloth from her grasp and began moving it energetically across her shoulders and down to her lower back. "You look good here in my shower. I could get used to the sight of you hanging around."

"Thanks. Don't say anything more; it may go to my head."

"On the mornings when I happen to wake up in your bed and use your shower, you'll have to remember to say something equally gracious," he told her smoothly, snapping the washcloth playfully at her rounded bottom.

"Ouch!" It was her turn to yelp. "That wasn't kind," she reproached him, her hands going to the injured portion of her anatomy.

"Remember the next time you decide to kick me that I always get even. Not mad, just even." Closing his eyes in contentment, Gage turned his face up into the water, effectively cutting off Rani's portion.

"Hey, you're stealing all the water!"

"Sorry, I'm not used to having to share," he returned honestly, opening his eyes again. His mouth edged upward. "And you're such a little thing, you could easily get lost here in the tub if I'm not careful."

"I'm not that small. You're just oversized."

"Last night," he reminded her quite gently, "everything seemed to fit perfectly."

She felt herself going as red as the tub for no good reason and hastened to step out of it, grabbing for one of the thick red towels. Firmly she closed the shower curtain on his interested expression.

Back in the bedroom she slipped into her black dress,

belting the leather sash with a wry expression not untinged with a flicker of excitement. The man was a barbarian in some respects, a conquering warrior of the old school. She must be crazy to be so enthralled with him!

Later, wearing jeans and a long-sleeved shirt with rolled-up sleeves, Gage puttered familiarly around the kitchen, fixing coffee and pointing out the location of eggs and toast. There was an unexpected ease about the way they managed to get breakfast ready between them.

"We do this as if we've been doing it together for years," Gage observed complacently as they sat down to the meal. He poured her coffee and handed her the cream.

"Bored with domestic routine already?" she teased, lifting the cup to her lips.

"On the contrary. I find it rather comfortable." He looked up and caught her gaze. "What about you?"

Not at all certain where this was leading, Rani hesitated and then spluttered as the strong coffee went down. "You may have been right about the coffee," she gasped, adding another dose of cream. "Definitely a secret weapon!"

He frowned. "Sorry. As I said the other day, I'm not used to fixing it for anyone else. But I can learn," he added cheerfully. He waited.

Rani faced him warily. She knew he was waiting for some further response and wasn't sure what that response was supposed to be. He saw the confusion in her and smiled.

"Honey, in a few days, when this Prescott business is behind us . . ." He broke off as she interrupted him with a silently arched brow. "Don't look at me like that. We are going to get it settled, you know. You're going to go back and satisfy Aaron Prescott."

"No."

"Damn it, don't sit there and say no like that! You're going back if I have to drag you by the heels. It's for your own good, you little idiot, can't you understand that?" he snapped, gulping the strong coffee in irritation.

Rani tried a bright smile. "Does this mean the affair is over already? I told you taking me to bed wasn't going to make any difference in my decision." But something inside her wasn't feeling very bright or breezy. Rani suddenly discovered she was growing rather anxious. She realized she definitely did not want the affair to end after only one night.

"The affair is not over!" Gage grated, glaring at her across the rim of his cup. "It's just begun, and as I was about to say before I was so rudely interrupted, in a few days—when you've gone back to Dallas and straightened everything out—I thought we might try living together."

Rani blinked, not knowing whether to be relieved or more cautious than ever. "Did you?"

"Look, I know neither of us is used to living with another person, and I'm not saying we should rush into that sort of setup without giving ourselves plenty of time. After all, we each have our own routines, our own way of doing things, and living together would be quite an adjustment for both of us. I understand that, believe me. But I think you and I might manage a cooperative effort, sweetheart," he concluded, his mouth softening as he regarded her intently.

"After I return from Dallas?" she clarified blandly.

"There's plenty of time."

Rani stared blindly down at her plate. "I'll, uh, give it some thought." She stood up abruptly. "Now I've really got to be on my way, Gage. I've got a number of things to do today and I imagine you do, too. . . ."

He didn't try to detain her. Instead he walked her out to the car when she was ready, leaning down to kiss her good-bye through the open window. "I'll see you later this afternoon, honey. We'll have dinner again. My treat this time."

"Fine." Rani accepted the order without pausing to think, anxious now only to escape from his presence long enough to sort through the mix of her emotions. Live with him? Was that what she wanted? Would that satisfy the strange uneasiness that had been coming and going all morning since she'd climbed out of his bed?

She drove back home, no nearer to an answer than she had been when she'd left Gage's side. Her mind was so occupied with the turmoil of her thoughts that she didn't notice her sister standing at her front door until she was in the drive.

"Rani! Where in the world have you been? I tried to call you last night and first thing this morning. I finally decided to drop by on my way to work and . . . What in the world . . . ?" Donna Cameron stopped short, staring as Rani got slowly out of the yellow Mazda. With an older sister's practiced eye she scanned the black dress, the high-heeled sandals and Rani's casually knotted hair. "I don't believe this! My little sister, who hasn't been serious about a man in five years, is coming home from a night out on the tiles?"

"Don't laugh at me, Donna. I've had a difficult morning." Rani allowed herself a wry expression as she fished for the apartment key.

"Preceded by a hard night?"

"It's not nice to tease your little sister." Rani pushed open the door, entering the sanctuary of her home with a feeling of vast relief. Everything was comfortable and known there. There she was definitely the one in charge.

"I'm not teasing you." Donna grinned. "At least, not much. To tell you the truth, I think I'm delighted. Shall I make you some coffee while you get properly dressed for the day?"

"Nice, mild coffee, please. And what the hell do you mean, you're delighted?"

"You were with Gage Fletcher, weren't you?"

"Does it matter?" Rani shot back, annoyed.

"I like him, Rani." Donna moved into the kitchen. "If it had been King Tanner, I would have grave doubts. But I think Gage is perfect for you."

"What's wrong with King?" Rani felt obliged to defend the absent cowboy. "And how do you know I was with Gage?"

"If you'd been with King, you would have been driven home in that rhinestone-studded Lincoln. Besides, I knew Gage was taking you out last night. He told me the day before yesterday when he stopped by the shop, looking for you, that he didn't intend to let you go out with King the Wonder Cowboy again."

"Did he indeed?" Rani snapped waspishly. "You two seem to have had quite a talk."

"We discovered we had a mutual interest. You."

A thought struck Rani and she paused in the doorway, her fingers splayed against the jamb, her tawny eyes darkening with anxiety. "During this little talk did you happen to mention that I'm going to be buying the shop, Donna?"

Her sister glanced up, surprised. "No. The subject didn't arise. Why?"

Rani shrugged. "I'd rather you didn't tell him, that's all."

"But why, Rani?"

"I just don't want the man knowing every aspect of my life." She pulled away from the door frame and started down the hall to change into jeans and a cotton knit shirt.

"But, Rani, why shouldn't he know?" With characteristic persistence Donna followed, watching as her younger sister stepped into the jeans and drew up the zipper.

"Forget it, Donna. But please don't let him know. It's important to me. I'll explain it all some other time." She snatched up the turquoise knit shirt and slipped it over her head before stuffing her feet into a pair of sandals.

"Okay, okay," Donna soothed. "I'll go finish the coffee."

Rani watched her leave the room and then glanced

down at the black dress lying on her bed. The leather
sash was draped menacingly across the folds of the
fabric. She knew now why she didn't want Gage to know
about her plans for buying The Miniature World. It was all
suddenly quite clear.

If he realized that her future was quite secure, he was
also bound to recognize that none of his basic arguments
would have enough leverage to force her back to Dallas.

There would no longer be any point in offering her
money to tide her over during the uncertain period
between jobs, and there would no longer be any point in
insisting that she needed Prescott's goodwill. In short, if
he knew she was buying The Miniature World and had
her future planned out, Gage would also know he could
give up on his task of trying to get her back to Dallas.

And until she knew for certain that he was truly
interested in her and would remain so even if the
business between them ended badly for him, Rani didn't
want him knowing how hopeless his task really was.

The realization that she was deliberately hiding that fact
from Gage made Rani uncomfortably aware of how
much she wanted him to stick around. She simply
couldn't bring herself to take the chance of discovering
that he was only interested in her because she was a job
for him.

She needed a little time, Rani decided as she went to
join her sister in the kitchen. A little time to be sure that
what she and Gage had between them was real and
would last once their business was concluded. She would
let him think that all he needed to do was to keep
arguing, keep pounding away at her defenses with
combinations of logic and financial incentive in order to
get her to return to Dallas. When she was more certain of
him and of herself, she would tell him the whole truth and
take the risk.

"Gage seems entranced with the miniature soldiers,"
Donna observed chattily as she poured coffee and sat
down at the kitchen table. "He has an amazing knowl-

edge of military history, though, so I suppose the military miniatures are a natural for him. It's a wonder he hadn't discovered them before."

"Yes." Rani honestly couldn't think of anything else to say to that. It was clear that Donna was quite taken with Gage Fletcher. "Did you get the photographer squared away yesterday?" Anything to change the subject!

"Finally! Lou and I must have gone to nearly half a dozen places, trying to choose just the right one, but we finally found it. It's a young couple and they do absolutely beautiful work. This will be the most stunning wedding album, Rani! I can't wait!"

Rani grinned at her sister's unabashed enthusiasm. "Maybe you should become a professional wedding planner when you move to Denver. You're certainly enjoying yourself with this one!"

"That's not a bad idea," Donna began seriously and then laughed. "Time enough to worry about that later. I'm just lucky at the moment that Lou is the patient type and willing to humor me while I plan the perfect wedding." Her smiling eyes narrowed thoughtfully at her sister. "I have the feeling Gage wouldn't be nearly as accommodating."

Rani started, her coffee cup rattling a bit as she replaced it in the saucer. "The issue doesn't arise and won't arise. Gage is not interested in marriage, and besides, the relationship isn't anywhere near serious enough to even think about it!"

"You spent the night with him, Rani."

"People do, occasionally, spend the night with each other!"

"Don't try to pretend it's a routine act on your part," Donna said firmly. "You know damn good and well it isn't! You've been dating King Tanner since you came back from Dallas, and I'd be willing to bet you still haven't gone to bed with him. You haven't seemed more than politely interested in a man for so long, I can't even remember the last time I would have said you were in love!"

"I am not in love," Rani declared stiffly, pouring herself more coffee. "How could I be? I . . . I hardly know the man. It's a matter of physical attraction," she wound up muttering. "Gage . . . Gage interests me."

"And for you that's a lot more dangerous than the comfortable, easygoing sort of love you've always sought, isn't it?" Donna observed perceptively. "You have been pursuing the wrong kind of relationship for so long that you're totally unprepared for the right one when it comes along!"

Rani was trying to think of a snappy response to that observation when the phone rang. Grateful for the interruption, she reached for the chocolate-brown wall phone.

"I've had a hell of a time finding you, Rani!" came a familiar masculine voice as she answered. "You sure did a neat disappearing act, didn't you? Dad was furious!"

Brady Prescott had tracked her down. Rani closed her eyes in dismay, picturing the handsome features of the thirty-year-old son of Aaron Prescott: Brown hair, hazel eyes and an underlying integrity that, she believed, would one day blossom into the strength of will that would enable him to step into his father's shoes. There were other Prescott family members scattered among the hierarchy of Prescott Services, all male, but Brady was the son and heir.

A confrontation with Brady was just what she needed to round out her day, Rani thought grimly.

6

〜〜〜〜〜〜〜〜

Prescott's son?" Donna echoed a few minutes later as Rani got off the phone. "How did he find you?"

"Said he finally remembered that I had a sister in Albuquerque. When he got into town, he called your answering service and they told him you might be at this number."

Donna's mouth curved apologetically. "I'm sorry, Rani. I'll have a word with the service. They certainly had no right . . ."

"It doesn't matter," Rani sighed. "After all, Gage had already found me."

"True. And if he can't persuade you to go back, I somehow doubt Brady Prescott will do it!" Donna chuckled. "Prescott must be livid by now. He thinks you seduced his son?"

"He's probably angry enough by now to accuse me of just about anything, but in his more rational moods I don't think Prescott would go quite that far. He just thinks Brady was a little too much under my influence. Aaron is a little old-fashioned," Rani muttered vengefully. "He thinks it's very dangerous for a man to be too much under the influence of a woman. Especially the man who is slotted to inherit Prescott Services, Incorporated."

Donna looked thoughtful. "Why did you give Brady your address?"

"Why not? As I said, I've already been tracked to my lair. What does it matter if Brady finds me, too?" Rani's mouth twisted in a brief parody of a smile.

"Why does he want to see you?"

"My guess is that he'll do the same thing Gage is trying to do: tell me to go back to Prescott Services. I have a hunch Brady is looking for a face-saving way back into the firm. If I return with him, he'll be able to convince himself it's all right to back down in front of his father on this issue. If he has to go crawling back alone and admit he's too weak to stand on his principles . . ."

Donna nodded. "I get it. You're the offended party, and if *you* back down, it won't look so bad for him to agree to accompany you back to Dallas. Not his fault the little woman gave in to pressure."

"Something like that. Probably." Rani considered that. "The boy may have more of his father in him than I first thought!"

"Well, I'm sure this is going to be a fascinating confrontation, but frankly, I think I'll excuse myself. I still have a business to run." Donna rose gracefully and carried her cup over to the sink. "I'll see you later, Rani. Give Gage a call if Prescott junior gets too annoying."

Rani frowned. "What good would that do? Gage wants the same thing Brady does. Have you forgotten? He wants me back in Dallas, too!"

"Somehow," Donna declared as she walked out the door, "I have a hunch Gage would rather do his own convincing."

She was gone before Rani could demand an explanation. With a disgusted sigh, Rani closed the front door and went back into her kitchen to clean up.

Less than forty-five minutes later Brady Prescott was ringing her bell. When she opened the door, she found his handsome features set in lines of grim concern. It wasn't long before she realized the concern was for himself as well her. Brady was in a bind.

"Rani, you've already taught Dad a lesson. Why not just go back and pick up where you left off? Doesn't the salary mean anything to you? You were making good money there. How are you supporting yourself now? Your savings? It's ridiculous to keep holding out when you've already accomplished your goal!"

Rani sprawled languidly on the sofa across from him and smiled blandly. "I'm not going back, Brady. But there's absolutely no reason you can't."

He glowered at her. "How's it going to look if I go back alone?"

"As if you've had second thoughts about walking out in the first place?" she suggested unkindly.

"Exactly!"

"That's not my problem. I never asked you to grand-stand like that. You should have thought about your own future, not mine."

"Damn it, Rani! I did it for you!"

"You did it as a way of taking a stand against your father. And that's all well and good, but when you take stands, you have to be prepared to stick by them."

"You have no right to sit there and give me moral lectures!" Brady's mouth twisted wryly. "Oh, hell, Rani. How was I to know you meant to stay away for good? I thought you'd just walk out long enough to make a scene and teach Dad a lesson."

"And then go crawling back?"

"It wouldn't be crawling!"

"A matter of opinion," Rani murmured and smiled sweetly. "I'm not going back, Brady, but you must do what you want to do."

The younger man hesitated and then warned carefully, "Dad doesn't like to be made a fool of. He won't sit still for this, Rani. He thinks you're going to steal the Henderson account, you know. He won't take that kind of retaliation calmly!"

"He's already tried his best shot at convincing me to go back and it hasn't worked. I don't see what else he can do." Rani lifted one shoulder in bland dismissal.

"What do you mean?"

"He sent someone after me to convince me to return and clean things up."

"Who?" Brady looked at her blankly.

"A man named Gage Fletcher."

"Fletcher!" Brady got to his feet, running a hand through his thick brown hair as he paced restlessly toward the empty fireplace. *"Fletcher!"*

"You know him?" In spite of herself Rani found she was tensed for the answer.

"I know *of* him. He's in the business security field, isn't he? Consulting and such?"

"Yes."

Brady shook his head once, as if trying to track down a vague memory. "I'm not sure what the relationship is with my father, but I think Dad has something on him."

"Has something on him? What in the world do you mean?" Rani stared at him, more shocked than she wanted to admit. She had been prepared to accept that Gage might have been hired by Prescott in the course of business, but the notion that Prescott might be using other kinds of pressure to force Gage to do his dirty work unnerved her.

"I don't really know the details, Rani. I've heard Dad speak of him a few times and I always had the impression he owed my father something. That he was somehow in debt to Prescott Services. You know Dad. He won't hesitate to call in a debt if he wants something done. He's quite willing to apply the pressure. God knows what kind of favor or money Fletcher must owe him."

Was that why Gage grew so angry every time she accused him of bounty hunting? This wasn't just a job for him; he was committed to succeeding because he was under some sort of obligation to Aaron Prescott. Rani's lips tightened. She didn't like the idea that Prescott was holding a weapon over Gage's head. It disturbed and angered her.

"Look, whatever the means Dad's chosen to use, I know him well enough to know they'll probably work. If Fletcher has been sent after you, it's because Dad is convinced the man won't quit until he succeeds. Dad must have a pretty good hold on him. Why go on fighting, Rani? Let's go back and pacify Dad. In the long run it will all be for the best. After all, I'm going to take over the reins of Prescott Services one of these days, and once I'm in charge, you can bet things will be different!"

Rani arched an eyebrow. "No one's stopping you from going back by yourself, Brady."

He swung around to glare at her, his temper clearly beginning to fray. It was obvious Brady Prescott had been under a great deal of pressure since he had chosen to flaunt his father's will, and now he wanted a way to get out from under the gun.

"You're not going to use me to smooth things over with Aaron," Rani advised gently.

He came toward her in two long strides, his good-looking face a mask of growing frustration and anger. Rani was so surprised at his unexpected surge of violence that she didn't even have a chance to get out of the way. Brady had reached down and hauled her to her feet in a matter of seconds.

"Stop it!" she hissed, angered but not alarmed. "What's the matter with you, Brady?"

"Maybe Dad was right! Maybe women do need a man around to tell them what to do! I put myself on the line for you, Rani Cameron, and now you're laughing at me! I tried to stand up for you and now you won't do the same for me. You owe me something for what I did by walking out behind you at Prescott Services!"

"I don't owe you a damn thing! I never asked you to do that for me!" she blazed, disdaining to struggle. "But I sure as hell hope the whole thing will serve as a good lesson for you. Never put yourself on the line unless you're prepared to go the whole distance!"

"Why you ungrateful . . . *female!* I'm beginning to think my father is right in more ways than one! Women shouldn't be allowed too much power. It goes to their heads! They belong in the kitchen and the bedroom!"

With that, Brady hauled her close in a punishing grip and plastered his mouth on hers in what was intended to be a severely chastising kiss. Halfheartedly Rani started to struggle, torn between using the passive resistance approach or outright defense tactics. Brady's embrace was radiating outrage and masculine frustration. Perhaps the best method of dealing with him in this mood was simply to let the waves of his emotions wash over her until he had worked out his anger.

She was still trying to analyze the situation and come up with the appropriate response when the decision was taken out of her hands. Literally.

"Let go of her or I'll break your neck."

Gage's low, gritted warning cut across the room with the impact of a whiplash. The effect on Brady Prescott was immediate and electric. He lifted his head, startled, to stare at the man who had just walked unnoticed through the living room door.

"Who the hell are you?" Brady's hands fell away from Rani's shoulders as he made the demand.

"The man to whom that particular woman happens to belong. And I'm not really a very generous soul. If you try taking another kiss, I'll take you apart. Have I made myself very clear?" The soft, mildly accented drawl was far more dangerous than any amount of yelling, Rani thought vaguely as she turned slowly to confront Gage.

He stood there holding a couple of boxes, the kind that housed miniature soldiers, dressed as she had last seen him, in close-fitting jeans and a white shirt. He wasn't looking at her; his whole attention was on Brady.

"Who is he?" the younger man snarled at Rani.

"Allow me to make introductions," Rani began with thinly veiled sarcasm. "Brady, this is Gage Fletcher. Gage, Brady Prescott. And now that the formalities have been observed, I shall take a minute to tell both of you what I think of your ridiculous, ludicrous and utterly appalling displays of machismo! Never in my life have I been subjected to such a scene, and I don't intend to start tolerating such events at this stage! Brady, you should be ashamed of yourself for quoting your father's philosophy on handling women! So much for your fine male libera-tion! And as for you, Gage Fletcher, I don't allow any man to act as if he owns me! How dare you barge in here without knocking and start threatening people!"

Neither man appeared overly concerned with her tirade. They were devoting their full attention to each other. Brady was wary and a little anxious. Gage was grim and coldly menacing.

"So you're Prescott's son." Gage's eyes scanned the length of the younger man with open disdain. "The one he thought had been dumb enough to find himself in the clutches of a scheming little hussy who only wanted to manipulate him for her own benefit!"

"Gage!" Rani nearly choked on the name. "If you think I'm going to stand here and let you insult me like that, you're out of your mind!"

"A minute ago you were claiming the 'scheming little hussy' for your own!" Brady snapped back as both men continued to ignore Rani.

Gage shrugged with eloquent unconcern. "Oh, I'm claiming her, all right. For better or for worse I made her mine last night. Ask her."

"Gage!" Rani's eyes widened in shock at the blunt words.

"Is that true?" Brady turned on her. "Have you been

to bed with him already? For God's sake, Rani, what's the matter with you? Are you going to let the man seduce you into going back to Dallas? Talk about not having the guts to stand by your principles! And you had the nerve to give me lectures on the subject!"

"Shut up! Both of you!" she raged, at the end of her patience. "I may not have the physical ability to throw either of you out the door, but I certainly don't have to stand here and listen to this male chauvinist drivel! I'm going for a swim. When I get back I want to find my home empty! Is that understood?"

Whirling on one heel, she strode toward the bedroom, slamming the door shut behind her. Once inside she grabbed the strapless maillot and then slammed back down the hall, departing through the kitchen door without sparing a glance for either of the men in her living room. Never had she been so incensed!

Who the hell did Gage Fletcher think he was to embarrass her like that? And what had gotten into Brady Prescott, acting like his father? Men! They were all alike under the surface. She changed in the small dressing room near the condominium-complex pool and went into the water with a flat dive that utilized all the energy of her anger. With long, gliding strokes she began doing laps in the nearly empty pool. Only a few other people were lounging nearby, settling in for a late morning tan beside the water.

For several minutes she let the cool water sap the heat of her outrage, and when she finally halted at one end, breathing quickly from her exertion, she looked up to see Gage sliding into the water beside her. He was clad in a pair of sleek red-and-white-striped swim trunks that hugged the shape of his lean, hard body to perfection.

"I figured we might go swimming today, so I brought along my suit," he told her blandly, idly sweeping his hands through the water in wide arcs as he stood facing her.

She stared at him, mute for a moment in the face of his unmitigated gall. How dare he act as if nothing had happened? Eventually she managed to find her voice. "What," she demanded in low, even tones, "did you do with Brady?"

"He's gone. I told him to go back home to Dallas and Dad."

"I see." Rani watched, seething, as Gage ducked briefly beneath the water to wet the remainder of his body. When he emerged, flipping his dark hair out of his eyes with a toss of his head, she tried again. "And he went?"

"As far as I know. At any rate he's not in your apartment any longer."

A purely male satisfaction at having so easily routed the opposition was emanating from him in waves. Rani could have slapped his tanned face. No wonder it was primarily men who waged war. It was the male of the species who had the arrogance to use violence or threaten to use it, and it was also the male of the species who was capable of deriving such satisfaction from victory. Women, Rani decided, were generally a far more practical lot. It wasn't that they were truly the gentler sex, merely more inclined to use a rational, intelligent approach to getting what they wanted—an approach not influenced so much by pride and the will to dominate.

"You should be ashamed of yourself, Gage Fletcher," she told him flatly.

"Why? I did the guy a favor. It's better to quell that sort of crush quickly. I used the most efficient technique I knew."

"Crush!"

"That's all it was, you know," he explained kindly. "Brady had a crush on you. His father was right to worry about your influence on his son. You would have led Brady a merry chase, to say the least, and Aaron would always have worried about you running Prescott Services instead of his son. Brady needs a chance to mature and learn to set his own standards and make his own decisions. With you around 'guiding' him it would have taken a great deal longer for him to come into his own power, and if you had actually married him, it might have taken forever!"

"Married him! I never had any intention of marrying him!"

"You and I know that," Gage said with a pacifying air, "but Aaron doesn't know that. Actually, once you settle the Henderson account, I think Prescott is going to bid you farewell quite cheerfully. He doesn't like threatening women. With his son safely back in the fold and the Henderson account no longer in danger of being stolen, I think he'll be quite pleased to have you off the premises!"

"And what about you, Gage?" she shot back, unable to restrain herself. "Will you be equally happy to collect your bounty money and get me off the premises?"

She saw the flare of anger in his gaze and wished immediately that she hadn't tried to goad him once more on that subject. Whatever Prescott's hold on Gage, it must be severe to induce such a fierce response every time it was mentioned!

"I'll be satisfied to have kept my word to Prescott," Gage replied tightly. "But I won't be kicking you out of my life. We have an arrangement, remember? An affair. And I haven't begun to satisfy myself in that regard. What's more, I think you're still a little unsatisfied, too!"

He reached out, catching her around the waist and dragging her toward him through the water.

"Gage, please! There are people around!"

"So what?" He leaned back against the side of the pool, separating his legs underwater and propelling her between them so that she was tightly molded to his thighs.

The intimacy of the far too public display made her gasp. Her palms flattened against his chest, nails digging into the tanned flesh. But the small punishment didn't slow him down. He kissed her with a thoroughness that brought knowing grins from the few sunbathers around the pool.

The aroused anger in him was far stronger than she was, and much to her own disgust Rani opted for submission as the better part of valor. She wanted no more scenes. Better to get this one over than stage an even bigger attraction for the discreet poolside voyeurs by engaging in an all-out battle.

Eventually, sensing victory, Gage lifted his head, the dangerous cast of his face modified into a less menacing, although far more infuriating, expression of satisfaction. His hands slid possessively down over her buttocks, anchoring her a moment longer against his hardness. God! He was letting her know that even in that short span of time he had become aroused by desire as well as anger. Did he want her so much?

"See what you do to me?" he whispered throatily, eyes gleaming. "If there weren't half a dozen people sitting around this pool at the moment, I'd drag you out onto the grass and make you finish what you've started! As it is, it's going to be a few minutes before I can get out of the water without embarrassing both of us! I think I'd better do a few laps."

He released her, gliding off through the water with long, powerful strokes that made his smoothly muscled back and shoulders ripple in the hot sun. Rani realized she was watching, fascinated. Her mind was filled with images of what it would have been like if they had been alone and Gage had made love to her in the grass beside the pool.

It was ridiculous. She ought to have been furious with him, and instead she was daydreaming with an intensity of passion she would never have thought possible.

They spent the major part of the day by the pool, drinking iced tea and lazily eating sandwiches that they made in Rani's kitchen. Considering its rather shaky start, this had evolved into one of the most sublimely pleasant days Rani had ever experienced. What was the matter with her? Her emotions were too complex to even begin to comprehend.

"I dropped by your sister's shop this morning on my way over to see you," Gage said as he emerged from the pool for the third time.

"I noticed you were carrying some of the boxes she uses for military miniatures." Rani looked up at him, eyes half closed against the sun.

"She loaned them to me for a couple of days. Instead of going out tonight I thought we might spend a quiet evening at home."

"If you think I'm going to let you trick me into another losing battle . . ."

He chuckled, sinking down onto the lounge chair beside her. "That would be unfair of me, wouldn't it? After all, you're already fighting so many losing battles."

"A matter of opinion!"

"Shall I make reservations for the day after tomorrow, Rani?" he asked softly.

"Reservations for what?"

"The trip to Dallas."

"You're determined to ruin this day one way or another, aren't you, Gage?" she drawled.

He drew in a long breath before saying carefully, "I've offered you the inducement of Prescott's money and I've pointed out the logic of placating him. You're not leaving me much in the way of alternatives, Rani."

Her lips curved in a half-smile of anticipation as she waited, eyes closed, for the next tactic. "What *is* left, Gage? Brute force?"

There was a distinct silence from the lounge chair beside her. And then: "You guessed it."

Rani's eyes snapped open and she turned her head to stare at him. Gage hadn't moved, his eyes hidden behind the silver and black of his sunglasses. "That's impossible and you know it," she challenged tensely. "You can't possibly drag me back to Dallas."

"Wanna bet?"

"This isn't a joke, Gage. Even if you managed somehow to get me there, which is highly unlikely, there's no way on earth you could force me to go to work once you had stuffed me back behind my desk!"

"I'm prepared to stand over you and make whatever threats are necessary. I have a feeling that once you're actually there, you'll do whatever needs to be done to get yourself back out. The easiest way of accomplishing that feat will be to tie up the Henderson account, tell Brady to do his filial duty and wave good-bye to Aaron Prescott with a polite smile."

"What exactly is Prescott going to pay you for pulling off a stunt like that?" she asked evenly.

"Damn it, Rani, will you forget about that angle? Once and for all, I'm doing this for your sake as much as anything else!" She knew he was watching her from behind the reflecting sunglasses but she couldn't see his eyes. She could imagine the grim determination that would be lighting them, however. And regardless of her burning curiosity, Rani couldn't bring herself to ask exactly what kind of favor Gage owed Aaron Prescott. What if it were something too terrible? Too private? Too embarrassing or humiliating for him?

"I suggest we change the subject," she finally said with false calm. "The present one seems to have deteriorated."

He let it drop—much to her surprise—and the afternoon wore on, slipping back into a lazy pattern that finally concluded with potato salad and hamburgers that Gage cooked on Rani's patio grill. Once again the task of fixing a meal seemed to divide itself easily between the two of them. Gage, she discovered, even knew how to load a dishwasher. Ah, the skills of a man who has lived alone!

After dinner he opened the boxes of miniature soldiers and began setting them up on the carpet in front of Rani's beautifully furnished dollhouse. She rearranged the exquisite furniture in the drawing room of the Regency mansion while he worked.

"What battle?" she asked, seeing him absorbed in organizing a group of redcoated infantry.

"Blenheim, 1704," he answered, tearing a strip of paper into a long, narrow ribbon. "That's the Danube River, which was protecting one French flank and that"— he scrawled the name Lutzingen on a piece of paper and dropped it near the other flank of French soldiers—"is one of the three towns the French tried to hold. The territory around it was pretty rough, so it protected the other flank. In the middle was the town of Oberglau and here near the Danube was Blenheim. The Comte de Tallard, the French commander, massed his cavalry between the towns. His only serious concern was the front. There was another river between his men and the British. The river Nebel. Much smaller than the Danube."

"And on the other side?" she prompted, setting down a tiny Regency chair and curling her legs under her to watch. "Who was in charge of the British?"

"The British troops were commanded by the Duke of Marlborough. A general who happened to be blessed with an incredible amount of common sense. He was one of the first to pay serious attention to such things as keeping his men rested and well fed. Maintaining supply lines has always been a problem in war, and he developed some special techniques for handling it. He was also one of the first to set high standards of drill and discipline for his troops."

"If this is going to be another lesson in military discipline," Rani began complainingly, "I don't think I want to listen!"

Gage's mouth edged upward as he bent over the task of setting out British cavalry. "No, it's just that I've always been curious about this particular battle. There was a point when the French could have won, but Tallard missed the crucial moment. I've always wondered what it looked like on the field."

Rani watched interestedly. "How did the British get the troops across the Nebel?"

"The engineers built five bridges. The infantry waded across and took up positions here and here until the bridges were finished and the cavalry was brought over. Marlborough and his ally, Prince Eugene, had decided to stage an assault over here on the town of Lutzingen. They wanted to draw strength away from the French center."

Rani watched the terribly harsh logic of the battle develop as Gage maneuvered the elegantly designed soldiers. The French artillery wrought damage to the British. The assault on Lutzingen made for rough going, and over at Oberglau the battle raged furiously.

Suddenly Rani frowned and leaned forward, her arms wrapped around her drawn-up knees. "There! The French just punched a big hole to the right of the British center. If they poured their cavalry through it . . ."

Gage glanced up at her, one brow arched in respect. "You, madam, have just shown yourself a hell of a lot more intelligent than poor Marshal de Tallard proved to be. That's the moment I spoke of earlier. The point where the tide of battle could easily have gone against the British. But the French commander apparently didn't have the excellent battlefront communications system Marlborough had established. Either that or he just didn't see the opportunity. Whatever the reason, Marlborough had time to sum up the situation and send for assistance from Prince Eugene. Between them they managed to close the gap in the line once more. By late that afternoon it was all over. Tallard surrendered. He probably never really stood much of a chance against Marlborough. He simply wasn't in the same league. Too weak and indecisive. The victory put a stop to the French plans to invade Italy and take Vienna."

A gap in the line. A weakness torn in an otherwise strong defense. Rani stared at the mock battlefield, thinking of the gap in her own defenses that had been rendered that morning.

Knowing that Gage was somehow in Aaron Prescott's debt was proving to be a dangerous point of weakness for her. A strange desire to protect this man from Prescott's undeniable ruthlessness was insidiously eating away at her resolve.

She was in no real danger from Aaron Prescott, but what about Gage? The notion was ridiculous, Rani tried to tell herself as she eyed the battlefield. If ever there was a man who could take care of himself, it was Gage Fletcher.

But if he'd somehow gotten himself into debt with Prescott and Prescott was calling in the tab, even Gage might be caught between a rock and a hard place.

She might be the only one who could rescue him. A gap in the line.

It was amazing what you could learn about human nature by studying warfare, Rani thought dryly. She would never have guessed the weakness in her line of defense.

7

~~~~~~~~~~~~~

Rani fiddled with the drawing room of her Regency dollhouse as Gage finally tumbled the miniatures back into their boxes. She felt strangely tense, not only because of the realization that she was weak where Gage was concerned, but because that realization made her uneasy about how the evening would end.

Gage, she knew, was assuming that the comfortable evening was going to end even more comfortably in bed. Her own whirling thoughts and mounting confusion made Rani shy away from that possibility.

She needed time to think. Time to sort out what was happening to her emotionally. When the last of the miniature boxes was snapped shut, she forced herself to look up and meet the smoky gaze that was now centered on her. What she saw there made Rani go cautiously still.

Gage was sitting on the floor with his back against the couch. He had one leg drawn up and was resting his arm negligently across it.

"Rani, I'm going to go ahead and make plane reservations for Dallas."

She had the feeling he'd been mulling over the sentence all evening, considering how best to tell her. Rani could have told him he'd wind up doing it very unsubtly. Gage Fletcher was not a subtle man. The words came out as a cool challenge. She found herself automatically responding in kind.

"Reservations for one, Gage?"

"For two. We'll go together," he stated.

"You're planning on taking me in handcuffed to the saddle?" She mocked him with narrowed eyes.

"Forget it, Rani, I'm not rising to your baiting cracks about bounty hunters. We're going back to Dallas for your own good, and if you weren't so damn stubborn, you'd acknowledge that. Come to think of it, because you *are* so damn stubborn, this may be the easiest way for you to go. After all, if I drag you back, you'll be able to tell yourself you never really gave in, won't you?"

"A little battlefield psychology?" she suggested dryly. Her fingers tightened around the small table she had been about to place in the drawing room. Carefully she set it down.

"A little male-female psychology," he corrected mildly.

Now is the time, she thought. Tell him there's no point in hounding you any longer. You're not going back to Dallas because you don't have to worry about appeasing Aaron Prescott. You've got another job all nicely lined up.

But this decision no longer involved only herself. Whatever she decided to do also affected Gage, and she had no way of knowing just how much it would affect him. She needed a little more time. If she used her secret weapon that night and he realized just how hopeless his task really was, he might give up and walk out the door.

Where would that leave him? Where would it leave her? It would be far more awkward to change her mind and go back to Dallas with everyone knowing she was only doing it for Gage's sake! It could be devastatingly humiliating for a man to have a woman rushing to his rescue like that. If she decided to go back, it would be far better for his male ego if everyone thought he had simply succeeded in his task.

"So now I'm faced with the last of your three weapons, is that it, Gage?" she murmured coolly. "Brute force?"

"Take your pick, Rani. Logic, money or force. Or all three, for that matter. It's not important to me which line of reasoning you select as long as you go back to Dallas and get Prescott off your back."

And off yours, she added silently. "Well, I can't stop you from making the reservations," she told him arrogantly, lounging back against the chair beside her.

"You'll be on the plane with me, Rani," he vowed softly.

She merely smiled. A very bright, very challenging, very feminine smile that completely hid her inner turmoil. It succeeded in provoking Gage as no amount of outright defiance could have done. In a smooth, flowing rush of easy strength he leaned across the short distance separating them and pulled her into his lap. She sprawled there helplessly, forced to lie along his thighs. The virile power in him was suddenly swamping her senses as the muscled legs cradled her while his hand came possessively down across one breast.

"Logic, money, force or *sex*, Gage? Is this the fourth method of persuasion?" she taunted, her body pulsating with the throbbing heat he was already beginning to arouse in her.

"No!" The denial was harsh and followed by a bluntly explicit oath. "I've told you this side of things is separate!" The hand cupping her breast slid down the turquoise shirt and up under the hem, seeking direct contact with her skin. She trembled as he found it, and Gage was immediately aware of her reaction.

"You'll have to forgive me if I get confused occasionally," Rani made herself say softly. His thumb grazed the tip of her breast, coaxing forth the eager nipple.

"Just do as I say and you won't get confused," he groaned, leaning over to kiss her with a harsh hunger. "Let me make the decisions for you, Rani."

"I've always made my own," she retorted as he shifted her into a more comfortable position. The defiance was automatic and instinctive. She really wasn't thinking about their war. She was thinking about making love instead.

"Not this time," he rasped. "Not this time." He was lying alongside her now, using one hand to press her along the length of his taut body. He cradled her head with his other arm, pinning her in place for his marauding mouth. The kiss was heavy and deeply sensual, as intimate as any actual lovemaking. It repossessed and reclaimed and left Rani shivering with reaction.

If she was ever going to buy herself some time to think, it had better be then, some remnant of common sense told her, and Rani knew she ought to listen. In a few more minutes she would be beyond thinking at all.

"Your offer to make my decisions for me is, of course, greatly appreciated," she got out throatily, trying to stiffen her body against his. "But I'm not quite ready to turn that part of my life over to you. In fact, tonight, I'm not willing to turn anything over to you! I think you'd better go, Gage."

His arms tightened suddenly, trapping her as he lifted his head to gaze down into her wide-open eyes. "You can't send me away, Rani."

"Yes, I can. I *have* to send you away. Don't you understand? You're pushing me, crowding me, resorting to threats. What can I do except send you away?" The strain showed in her voice now and he heard it. For some reason it got through to him far more than her words.

"Easy, honey. Don't get yourself all worked up over it. It's going to be all right, sweetheart. Just relax and let me handle everything." His fingers massaged the nape of her neck with a gentleness that had nothing to do with passion.

"Touching me like that is only going to make me more nervous," she muttered caustically, struggling to sit up. "Good night, Gage."

He hesitated and she knew he was debating the issue in his mind. If he flatly refused to go, Rani knew very well they'd wind up in bed together. How would she be able to resist? But he got slowly to his feet and she realized that he'd made the decision to leave. Her small sigh was a mixture of relief and dismay.

Reaching down, he tugged her up beside him, holding both of her hands against his chest as he stared into her taut features. "I'll go, Rani. But it doesn't change anything between us, either the business or the personal side. I'll give you until tomorrow to come to terms with both. But tomorrow night I'll be in your bed, and the day after you'll be back in Dallas. *And don't make the mistake of thinking one has anything to do with the other!*"

Rani blinked anxiously, aware that he meant that last sentence with every ounce of his not inconsiderable will. He was determined to keep the two battles separate. On the one hand it was reassuring, implying, as it did, hope for their "arrangement." But it still left her with the problem of whether or not to go back to Dallas.

His mouth came down on hers before she could summon up an appropriate response, and he left her with his brand on her lips as he turned and walked out the door. He snatched up the boxes of military miniatures en route.

Shakily Rani closed the door behind him and sagged back against it. There was no longer any real choice. She would have to go back with him to Dallas. Whatever it was that Aaron Prescott was using as a hold over Gage Fletcher, she wanted her lover out from under it.

Slowly she straightened away from the door and headed down the hall toward her bedroom. And for

Gage's sake, she would not let him know that he was the sole reason for her decision to go back. It would be best if he simply thought one of his arguments or the combination of all three had worked. Her secret weapon would never be used.

Because if Gage understood that she was only going back to Dallas to protect him, he was likely to be furious. A man like Gage Fletcher would not easily tolerate the humiliation of having a woman try to protect or rescue him.

The realization that she cared enough about a man to be so concerned with his ego was startling. At the doorway of her bedroom Rani paused, staring blankly at her neat bed. She had never been so concerned about a man's stupid macho pride in her life! Up to that point she had occasionally made use of her knowledge of the vulnerable male ego to manipulate a man, but she had never gone out of her way to protect it!

And what did that signify? What kind of relationship was she getting herself into?

Her head spinning with uneasy and unsettling questions, Rani crawled slowly into bed, pulled up the covers and told herself firmly to go to sleep. She was the one who needed protection, she chided herself. Gage was going to be unstoppable the next day. With two deadlines running out, he would be moving back and forth across the battlefronts like lightning.

It was the ringing of the telephone that awoke her the next morning, and Rani's day did not get off to a good start when she discovered that the person on the other end of the line was King Tanner. The time had come, she thought, to make it clear that she was not a good marriage prospect. Poor King, he had refused to read all the early warning signals. He wanted a wife and he had pointedly refused to take any hint that Rani wanted only a casual dating relationship.

Standing beside the chocolate-brown wall phone, dressed in a robe, hair tumbling loosely around her shoulders, Rani tried to awaken herself sufficiently to deal with the delicate task of telling King that she was not going to be seeing him any more.

Perhaps, she thought as she eventually hung up the phone and began making coffee, she would have continued to see King a while longer if it hadn't been for Gage. After all, Tanner was agreeable company for the most part, and he hadn't yet begun to push for a more intimate relationship. Yes, it might have gone on for a few more dates, but Gage had made that impossible. Rani winced as she started the automatic drip coffee maker. Gage made it impossible to even think of dating another man.

King had taken her kind but firm refusal of another date like the western gentleman he was. After all, they both knew he was considered an excellent catch; there would be women waiting in line to pick up where Rani had left off. Gage, she thought as she poured out the coffee, wouldn't have taken refusal nearly as politely.

Well, now that she had one major task out of the way, she had better get on with the next difficult chore. Dressing again in her jeans and a western-cut shirt of off-white, natural cotton, Rani knotted a bright yellow scarf around her throat and climbed into the Mazda to tell her sister about her change in plans.

Donna had the shop open by the time Rani arrived and was busily going through the morning routine. "Oh, hi, Rani. I don't suppose you'd feel like working in the shop this afternoon? Lou just called and we're going to go looking for tuxedos."

"Sure." Rani smiled indulgently. She leaned against the counter as her sister finished setting up the cash register. "But I'm going to be, uh, unavailable for a few days after today, Donna."

Donna's eyes swung to her. "What's up?"

Rani sighed. "Promise you won't laugh? I'm going back to Dallas."

Donna let out a long whistle, brows lifting in amusement. "Well, I can't say I'm astounded by that news. I had a feeling Gage was going to succeed where other men might have failed!"

"Older sisters are supposed to be sympathetic, not go around saying 'I told you so'!"

Donna lifted one shoulder negligently. "You don't need my sympathy. Gage will take good care of you. So when the money and logic didn't work, he tried seduction, hmmm?"

"No!" Rani stiffened, her brows drawing together in a quelling frown. "The seduction had nothing to do with my decision to go back!"

"Then why are you going back, Rani?"

"It's difficult to explain. . . ."

"No, it's not." Donna smiled understandingly. "You're going back to please Gage, aren't you?"

Rani let out a long sigh. "Something like that, I suppose." That was the understatement of the year! She was going back to protect her lover from some unknown threat, but perhaps Donna was half-right. Even without the threat hanging over Gage's sable head, Rani had a feeling she would still have been boarding the plane the following day.

"Oh, Rani, you little idiot. You've never gone out of your way to please a man in your life! Especially not to the extent of forsaking something you wanted. And you certainly wanted to see Aaron Prescott squirm a little, didn't you?"

"It would have been pleasant. He sure deserves it!"

"But you'd rather please Gage than take a little satisfaction at Prescott's expense. Doesn't that tell you anything about yourself?"

"It tells me I may be growing feebleminded," Rani acknowledged.

Donna laughed. "Well, if that's the case, it's a lucky thing you've got Gage around. That man is anything but feebleminded! You should have heard him talking strategy and tactics with one of the customers yesterday morning."

"I know. He's good for business," Rani murmured brightly.

"I like him, Rani. He's going to be good for you, not just business. You need a man who is as strong as you are. One you can argue with and who will stand his ground. You've always been so careful to choose males who won't give you any trouble that you've missed finding a man who was able to stand up to you and occasionally make sure you lost!"

"I hate battling relationships! You of all people should know that! How many times did I crawl into bed with you when we were little and stay there until Mom and Dad had finished quarreling?"

"I know their relationship was a little hard on us at times, but we just never really understood how it was with them. Conflict frightens children. But we're adults now, and I think it's time you realized that not all conflict between men and women is bad. You, for one, need a bit of it, if you ask me."

"I didn't."

"True, but as an older sister I've got some rights," Donna said, grinning. "And I'm using them to tell you that with a personality as strong as yours and with an independent streak like the one you've got, you need a man who's equally strong. Not one who won't draw the line occasionally."

"Don't yell at me; I've had a hard morning."

"Another one?" Donna demanded bluntly.

"Not because of Gage. King called me first thing this morning. I had to tell him I couldn't see him again."

"No loss. For either of you," Donna concluded forcefully. "That man would have driven you out of your skull in another month, and you would never have suited him, either. He could never have made you into a rancher's wife."

"You think I'm getting too old to be adaptable?" Rani grimaced.

"I don't think you'll make yourself adaptable for any

man except the right one. You've been on your own too long, and it will take a very special man to convince you to take the risk of giving up your freedom."

"The way Lou has convinced you to give up yours?" Rani shot back perceptively.

"I suppose I deserved that," Donna groaned. "But yes, that's exactly what I mean. After that fiasco of an elopement when I was just out of my teens, I wasn't sure I ever wanted to try marriage again. Poor Carl. It wasn't his fault. We were both so young and I was looking for a way to leave home."

"Because Mom and Dad's quarreling got to you, too?"

"Listen, Rani, let me tell you something. What Mom and Dad have between them may be loud at times but it's not real hostility! I found out what genuine husband-and-wife battles are when I married Carl! Believe me, there's a big difference!"

Rani thought about that. "You mean that, don't you?"

Donna nodded. "I certainly do. For Mom and Dad the passion sometimes slips over the edge and invades some of their, uh, discussions. But that's all it is. With Carl the quarreling was destructive and hopeless. When he took to drinking, there wasn't any chance left for either of us to make things work."

"But now you've found Lou."

Donna smiled, her happiness glowing in her eyes. "And this time it's right. And that, my dear sister, is why I'm so determined to have all the trappings right, too!"

"I think Lou understands why it means so much to you."

Donna nodded. "He does. But believe me, if he weren't willing to indulge me in this, I wouldn't insist on it. He's much too important to me. You, I think, will find yourself swept off your feet without any time for all the wedding hoopla," she added wisely. "Just a quick ceremony in some minister's office, I expect."

Rani swallowed uneasily, shaking her head. "I've told you, Donna, Gage isn't interested in marriage. And neither am I, for that matter," she added with a grim touch of bravado.

"I think you and Gage Fletcher have a surprise in store," Donna retorted. "Both of you are closet romantics, you know."

Rani arched an eyebrow disbelievingly. "Whence cometh that great piece of sisterly wisdom?"

"As far as Gage is concerned, it comes from watching him play toy soldiers," Donna shot back smugly.

Rani stared at her blankly. "What?"

Donna laughed, delighted at having stunned her younger sister. "Rani, I've been running this shop a long time and I've seen the kind of men who become involved in military history to the extent that Gage is involved in it. The clues to his romanticism are all over the place."

"What clues, for heaven's sake?" Rani found herself nearly shouting.

Donna raised her hand and ticked off her list of reasons. "Number one, he avoids twentieth-century warfare models like the plague. Why, do you suppose?"

"Too realistic. The blood is too real," Rani said slowly, remembering the brief discussion she'd had with him on the subject.

"Exactly. He prefers the fantasy element. The exciting, emotional, glorybound side of warfare. In other words, the *romantic* side of it. A lot of the customers are like that, as you'll learn. It's much easier to fantasize about long-ago battles, which always seem so much more heroic and bold in retrospect than the real-life mud and blood of a more modern battlefield. And reason number two," she went on as Rani looked at her in astonishment, "is that he likes to know and understand the emotional and intellectual sides of the various commanding officers involved in a conflict. I overheard him talking to one of my customers yesterday and you should have heard how passionate they became about the way Washington turned a rabble of farmers into a victorious army capable of defeating trained British professionals at Yorktown."

"That's the sum of your fine reasoning?" Rani felt obliged to mock. "You're generalizing about Gage's emotional makeup based on his hobby?"

"I could make a few generalizations about yours based on the same line of reasoning," Donna tossed back lightly. "After all, how many unromantic, cool business women do you know who collect Regency dollhouse furniture?"

"Stop right there!" Rani declared, holding up a warning hand. "I don't want to hear another word of your ridiculous assumptions and generalizations. Only a *romantic* like yourself could have drawn all those crazy conclusions. Go look for tuxedos."

Donna grinned. "I'm on my way. You'll notice I'm beginning to lose interest in my shop already? Can't wait to get to Denver!"

"Uh-huh. That's why you're drawing out this wedding for two months."

"I have never had so much fun in my life, Rani Cameron. We romantics take our pleasures in the oddest places."

Rani watched her leave with mixed feelings. With everything else that was on her mind, however, the last thing she wanted to do was mull over her sister's crazy ideas about Gage. Besides, she told herself grimly, the romantics of the world shouldn't try to paint everyone else in the same rosy colors. She and Gage were different than Donna and Lou, although that didn't mean they couldn't be quite happy in their own way.

How very prosaic that sounded! And at the moment she didn't feel at all prosaic.

The day proved a busy one for The Miniature World, and Rani was grateful for the activity. It kept her mind off the evening to come, when she would tell Gage she was going to go back to Dallas. She knew he would probably see her decision as a victory, and that annoyed her. On the other hand, she couldn't bring herself to tell him the real reason for her capitulation. Not a pleasant situation, given her somewhat hostile feelings toward the male sex at the moment.

She was just turning the Closed sign around on the front door when the black Jaguar pulled up at the curb. Gage's lean and massive frame got out with an easy masculine grace that made Rani simply stand and watch for a few seconds. What an effect he had on her senses, even from that distance!

Then he was at the door, politely waiting for her to unlock it. "I've got my own car, Gage. I don't need a ride home," she began hurriedly, saying the first words that came into her mind. He seemed a little larger that night, a little more intimidating for some reason. Probably psychological, she told herself briskly. She knew she was going to come out of whatever happened that evening looking like a loser, and that was affecting her judgment.

"I'll take you home," he said smoothly, stepping past her into the shop. "Finish locking up. Then we'll be on our way. We have a lot to do tonight."

"We do?" She slid him a deeply suspicious glance, uncertain of his mood.

"Yes."

"Gage, I can drive my own car home."

"It's safe enough in the parking lot. We'll get it in the morning before we go to Dallas."

Rani's mouth went dry for no discernible reason. She shut it, however, and proceeded to lock up, watching warily as Gage calmly pulled a couple of miniature-soldier boxes from under the counter. "Do you think Donna will mind if we borrow these this evening?" he asked, seeing her eyes on him.

"No, no, I don't think so."

"Good. Shall we be on our way?"

"Gage . . ."

"Let's go, Rani."

It was like trying to stem the tide of war, she thought wistfully as he bundled her into the Jaguar and drove off toward her apartment. Gage, as she'd sensed he would, had decided to make the final battlefield charge, and there was nothing she could do to stop him. Rani thought about telling him that she was going back to Dallas without further argument and decided it would be a superfluous statement. He already knew she was going back to Dallas because he'd made up his mind that she was.

They cooked dinner together in her kitchen, sharing the task once more. But as they sat down to eat the salad and the fettuccini with brown butter, Rani had the impression that Gage was laying careful plans for the evening. When he reached over to pour her another glass of the deep ruby California Merlot wine, she was sure of it. She was acutely aware that her conversation had been stilted for the most part since he'd picked her up at the shop. Perhaps he thought the wine would relax her somewhat?

He still had not brought up the subject of Dallas, and by the time the dishes were done, Rani felt distinctly on edge. She wanted to tell him quite calmly and matter-of-factly that she had changed her mind and decided to accompany him back to Texas, but Gage was making that impossible to do. There was some sort of war going on, and Rani couldn't even figure out where the battle lines were drawn.

He was polite, gracious and oh, so sure of himself. The combination made Rani increasingly annoyed. In the morning, she thought finally as they went into the living room, I'll let him know at the last minute that I'm willing to get on the plane.

It seemed quite natural to sink down onto the carpet again, Rani in front of her dollhouse, Gage with his boxes of soldiers. But out of the corner of her eye Rani watched him lay out a battle scene, and she didn't care for the grimly determined set of his hard mouth. Nervously she fiddled with the interior of the small Regency ballroom and wondered what was going on in his mind.

But he was absorbed in his project and slowly Rani

relaxed, idly adjusting a tiny rug in one of the small rooms. Donna's words came back to her as she carefully placed a tiny chest next to a canopied bed in a bedroom. What was it about the beautiful Regency dollhouse that really fascinated her? Why did she find a quiet contentment sitting there, playing with dollhouse furniture?

And why was she wondering rather wistfully what it would be like to create a real home for herself and a man who loved her? It wasn't the first time that she had sat in this position and thought such thoughts, but they had never been as poignant as they were tonight.

But Gage wanted an affair, not a real home. Rani forced herself to remember that and tried to convince herself that it would be enough. After all, both of them were mature adults, set in their ways and comfortable in their own routines. Wasn't it a little too late to be thinking of creating a real home?

Perhaps those instincts never died out in a woman, she decided as she toyed with the breakfast room. Perhaps the urge to make a home with a man was too primitive, too fundamental ever to be completely erased, no matter how long a woman waited to find the right man.

The right man. How, she asked herself for the hundredth time, could Gage Fletcher be the right man? Surely this nesting instinct should have arisen with someone like King Tanner, not Gage! Forcefully Rani pulled her thoughts away from the lure of the dollhouse.

"I can tell from the gorgeous French uniforms that you're doing a battle from the Napoleonic era," she ventured at last. That got his attention, at least.

"Waterloo." Gage placed a beautifully molded piece of field artillery into position. "And you're right about the uniforms. Napoleon had a fetish for glorious uniforms. He was always having new ones designed for the army."

"Donna says that's one of the reasons collectors like miniatures from that period. Lots of color and variety."

"And lots of battles," he reminded her.

"Yes." She glanced at her dollhouse, which was from roughly the same period as the Battle of Waterloo. The ballroom made her think of something. "Is it true Wellington danced the night away at the Duchess of Richmond's ball on the eve of Waterloo?"

"Wellington didn't believe in panic," Gage said dryly. "Yes, it's true. Come here, Rani."

She hesitated uncertainly, sensing a heightening of tension in the atmosphere. Damn! What she wouldn't give to be able to read his mind that night! "Why?"

"We're going to fight a battle, you and I." He sat back, surveying the field he'd constructed.

"Waterloo?" Her mouth twisted wryly.

"Ummm. Come here, Rani," he said again, glancing up to meet her suspicious gaze. His own eyes gleamed with a steady, very assured light.

"If we're going to fight Waterloo, I get to be the Duke of Wellington," she muttered, obeying the summons slowly.

"Not a chance," he told her with a small smile of satisfaction. "You're going to be Napoleon. Don't worry, you'll have help losing the battle." He picked up a miniature figure. "Marshal Ney. Unpredictable, hot-tempered and capable of some appallingly bad judgment. As one of Napoleon's commanders, he did his part in helping to lose Waterloo."

"Thanks!"

"This is the last day of the battle. The British arranged the infantry in squares like this. It made a rather solid battle formation."

"Are you sure I can't be Wellington?" she asked wistfully.

"Not tonight, Rani. Not tonight."

So she was forced to take the losing side, but even knowing the historical outcome, Rani couldn't help being caught up in the drama of despair, courage and glory that Gage outlined as they went along. Her French horsemen were hurled against the solid British fighting squares at a terrible cost to both sides. Marshal Ney's order for reinforcements was misinterpreted. Napoleon seemed out of touch with what was going on—not surprising, considering the clash and din of battle, but fatal.

Wellington, who believed firmly in centralized control and kept himself well informed via an excellent messenger system, held his lines until his Prussian allies arrived. By late evening, the surviving French were in full flight.

Rani looked up from the battlefield, leaving Napoleon to flee on his own. She had her own surrendering to do, and here in the aftermath of the devastating battle she, too, would lay down her weapons. There was no point in waiting until morning.

"What's Wellington doing now?" she asked whimsically.

"Writing his Waterloo dispatch. Letting the folks back in England know that it was all a rather close-run thing."

"Yes, it was, wasn't it? I'm going to Dallas with you in the morning, Gage."

Gage raised his head, confronting her from the victorious British side. "There really isn't any other choice, is there?"

"No." If he only knew how strangely little choice there had been!

"Trust me, Rani. It's best this way." He put out a hand and swept aside the remains of miniature soldiers and artillery. "I know it's hard to swallow your pride and I know how much you'd like to teach Prescott a small lesson. I also can guess that it probably isn't easy for you to surrender to me on this matter. But it will be okay, sweetheart; I'll take care of everything."

She looked at him, heard the determination in his low voice and then her lips edged upward in a wry smile. "Are the victorious generals always so polite to the losers?"

"I doubt it. I know they sure as hell don't make a practice of making love to the losers after the battle!"

Eyes glinting, Gage caught her hand and tumbled her lightly down onto the carpet, lowering himself alongside her. "But that skirmish is over, and we now have a much more interesting war to fight."

Did men only understand one sort of victory over a woman?

8

〜〜〜〜〜〜〜〜〜

It's all going to be for the best, Rani," Gage murmured, moving against her. His legs tangled with hers, trapping her as he anchored her wrists gently on either side of her head and leaned down to brush the contour of her throat with his lips. "Six months from now, when you're secure in a new position, you'll be glad you took my advice and didn't totally alienate Prescott."

"Took your *advice?*" she repeated breathlessly. "Is that what you call it?" A polite word for surrender!

"Well, maybe I have pressured you a little," he allowed. "But someone had to make you see sense! You were so determined to punish Prescott, you weren't thinking straight."

"You could be right about that last part," Rani agreed. She freed one hand to reach up and circle his neck. "I'm not at all sure I'm thinking straight!"

"Rani! My God! How I want you." A husky groan of rising desire muffled the words, but Gage's meaning was more than plain. He speared his hands into her hair, holding her head still for his kiss. Rani moaned once as he drove deeply into her mouth, and then she was yielding to him with grace and passion.

He took what she offered, allowing her free access to his own secrets in return. Rani's tongue teased lightly at the edge of his lips, her teeth wreaking a tiny havoc there before she plunged into the warmth of him. The thrill of desire spread to all their senses, igniting the passion that seemed to hover just below the surface.

Gage's voice was rasping as he tore his mouth free to trace an erotic pattern down to the opening of her shirt. "I feel as though I have to tie up all the loose ends tonight. I want to bind you to me so that when we get on that plane for Dallas, I'll know you won't be tempted to change your mind or run. Sweetheart," he muttered thickly, "sweetheart, do you know what I'm trying to say?"

"You've won, Gage, isn't that enough?"

"Not nearly enough! But I'll take what I can get and work on securing the rest," he vowed.

His hands moved over her, undressing her there on the carpet. In the space of only a few heated moments Rani lay naked and vulnerable, her hair tangled invitingly and her body curving toward him. He touched her with probing wonder, exploring the softness of her breasts and the gentle thrust of her hips. When she began fumbling with his clothing, Gage pulled away for a moment, tugging off the garments with impatience. Then he came back down beside her, his body hard and taut.

The sensual tension escalated rapidly. Rani's oversensitized skin felt seared wherever Gage touched her. When his fingers circled a budding nipple, she arched unthinkingly and whispered his name as her teeth sank lightly into his shoulder. Her hands trailed across the expanse of his back, now clinging, now dancing, until he responded with a muttered word of warning that sent waves of excitement cascading through her.

She felt the masculine power in him pushing at her,

threatening to overtake and conquer as it had once before. It elicited a strange mixture of emotions in Rani, a desire to fight and a desire to surrender. For some reason she couldn't seem to distinguish between the two, knowing only a curious need to struggle when it was far too late to do so.

"Lie still," Gage growled as he moved to cover her body with his own. But Rani's gilded eyes taunted him as she twisted aside.

"You think you can have anything you want from me, don't you, Gage? But there are still some things you don't know about me."

"Why are you trying to provoke me now?" he demanded hoarsely. "You belong to me, witch. You can't escape tonight." He thrust his leg between hers, forcing apart her silky thighs. The throbbing hardness of him menaced the vulnerable heart of her desire. Rani writhed beneath him, mocking him with her gleaming gaze.

"No, Gage, that's enough. You've won too many battles tonight. I don't think I want to let you win this one, too." But her voice taunted instead of protested.

His eyes were cloudy with the smoke of aroused passion as he looked down at her. "You seem to forget, you're the prize I won. All victors get to take their pick of the plunder, and the losers have no choice but to surrender it!"

His roughly haired leg moved along the inside of her thigh with exciting menace, and Rani gasped, clutching at his shoulders. Her head fell back across his arm, exposing her throat, and Gage took full advantage of the opportunity. She shivered as he nipped the delicate flesh at the pulse point he located so unerringly, and she cried out as he went from there to her breasts with gently marauding teeth.

"Gage! Oh, Gage . . . !"

"Tell me," he urged, letting her feel the promise of him. "Tell me you belong to me tonight!"

"Why should I?" she baited him, knowing that it was the truth and aware that he knew it also.

"Because I need to hear it, sweetheart," he surprised her by admitting. He slid down her body, touching the tip of his tongue to the hollow of her stomach and then tenderly feathering her thighs. Rani trembled beneath the sensuous assault and gave up the small battle she had been waging. "Say it, Rani!"

"Yes, Gage. Yes, *please!* I belong to you. *Make* me belong to you!" Her hands locked in his sable hair, pulling him up along her body as the need for him surpassed the need to tease and torment.

When he paused for a few tingling seconds to gaze down into her face again, Gage saw that the mocking light in her eyes was gone, leaving behind the genuine demand for fulfillment. "Some other time," he promised huskily. "Some other night you can taunt me and play games, but not tonight. Tonight you must know you're mine."

Without pause he surged against her softness, filling, taking, claiming. Rani's breath died momentarily in the depths of her throat as her body adjusted to the passionate male invasion. She was given little chance to absorb the impact of him. Gage simply swamped her, carrying her away on a tide of desire that left her no choice but to cling to him.

Rani did so, her nails digging into his skin, her legs wrapped tightly around his hips. She buried her lips against his throat and let her body succumb to the pounding strength that strove to master it.

Gage held her in a viselike grip, locking her body to his. Relentlessly he built the tempo between them, lifting her to a plane where his name was the only word that could get past her lips. She shimmered in his arms and he gloried in the heat of her.

"Gage!"

"Take me with you, sweetheart. Take me with you!"

No sooner were the words out of his mouth than her body went rigid with the final tremor. Rani clutched at him mindlessly, and together they spun through the culmination of their passion. She was distantly aware of Gage's fingers clenched tightly into her buttocks—knew the feel of his skin beneath her scoring nails—but little else intruded as they drew each other across the boundaries that separate human beings.

They rode the soft darkness of the aftermath together, sinking slowly back into reality on the carpet, entwined in each other's arms.

"Rani, Rani, you're so perfect for me. So perfect." Gage crooned the words over and over in her ear as his large frame lazed across her sprawled body. "So perfect."

When she opened her eyes at last, it was to find him watching her, his head nestled beside hers on the carpet. She could read the satisfaction in his expression and wrinkled her nose. "I warned you the last time about gloating!"

"A man's entitled to his little pleasures," he drawled teasingly, brushing her cheek with his mouth. His fingers toyed with the peak of her breast.

"Little pleasures!"

"Fighting wars is hard work," he defended himself. "Don't you want me to have a bit of satisfaction at the end of a rough day?"

"Is that all it was? A bit of satisfaction?" she mocked dangerously, twisting her fingers into the curling hair on his chest and tugging.

"Ouch! No, by God! It was not just a bit of satisfaction. You want the full truth? You make me feel the way Wellington must have felt after Waterloo, the way Washington must have felt after Yorktown, the way Marlborough did after Blenheim, the way . . ."

"Enough!" She stopped the words with her fingers, but that didn't stop the gleam of satisfaction and contented mastery in his eyes. "I knew it was a mistake to let you

drag me into a reenactment of Waterloo tonight." But her
eyes were smiling up at him, full of her own satisfaction
and contentment.

"Did you have a choice?" he drawled.

"You're supposed to be gracious and humble in
victory, Gage Fletcher. Not overbearing and arrogant."

"I'm sorry. I'll try to behave better next time," he
promised lightly, smoothing the tendrils of hair back from
her face in a possessive gesture.

"Next time?" She eyed him askance.

"Ummm. And the time after that and the time after
that and . . ."

"You're insatiable," she groaned, coiling her leg lightly
around his thigh.

"You're incredible," he countered, touching the tip of
his tongue to the hollow of her shoulder. "And you're
mine."

"Gage?"

"Hush, darling, I'm planning my next campaign." He
traced an exquisite little pattern across her stomach and
lower.

"No more rape and pillage on the battlefield," she
protested, squirming beneath him and wincing as her
rounded bottom rubbed across the carpet. "The loser
demands a real bed if there's going to be a next time. This
carpet leaves a little something to be desired in the way of
padding!"

He grinned suddenly and rose to his knee, bending
down to scoop her up into his arms. "Never let it be said
I'm not generous in victory." Without a backward glance
at the scattered soldiers and weapons left behind, Gage
carried her away from the scene of battle, into the dark
intimacy of her bedroom. Arms wrapped around his
neck, Rani closed her eyes and surrendered to what
remained of the night.

The sunlight that woke her the next morning brought
with it the reality of what lay ahead that day. Stirring
slowly beside the massive warmth of the man who lay

next to her, his arm slung possessively across her breasts, Rani yawned and blinked herself into full wakefulness. In a few hours she would be back in Dallas, and before she made one move toward straightening out the Henderson account, she was going to have Aaron Prescott's sworn promise to free Gage from whatever hold he had over him.

That resolve tightened her mouth and brought a cool, almost remote look into her tawny eyes. She had made her decision and she would stand by it, but she vowed she would get what she wanted from Prescott. And what she wanted was Gage's freedom.

"Good morning, Rani." Gage's lashes lifted lazily as he studied the profile of the woman beside him. The firm resolve and the remote wariness in his lover's face would have been obvious even to a blind man. Gage's own eyes narrowed with determination. "I think we'd better get going. The plane leaves in three hours and we still have to pack."

Hardly a romantic greeting, Rani thought in annoyance as she obediently flung back the covers and reached for her robe. But then, Gage had another kind of war to finish that day. Did he think she might try to back out of her promise to go with him to Dallas? Her irritation drove her toward the bathroom without a backward glance at the man who dominated her bed. She was doing this for his sake, damn it, although he couldn't be blamed for not realizing that. Someday, when the relationship had deepened to the point where she could be sure of not humiliating him, she might tell him exactly why she was going back to Dallas with him.

"Rani!" he called roughly when she reached the door of the bathroom. She ignored it and went inside to turn on the taps in the shower. A moment later the door reopened behind her with a small crash. "Rani, you're not going to change your mind. You're coming with me on that plane to Dallas."

On the point of stepping under the shower, Rani gave him a searching look. It was tempting to hurl another "bounty hunter" accusation at him, but she resisted and ducked out of sight behind the curtain instead.

"Damn it, woman, don't play games with me this morning!" He snatched the curtain aside, standing naked, legs braced slightly apart on the tiled floor. The hard lines of his face were set in a resolute expression, and there was aggressive command in every contour of his large, lean body. Hands on his narrow hips, he fixed a determined stare on her as she turned her face up to the water. "Do you hear me, Rani? You're going back to Dallas."

"I hear you, Gage. My neighbors probably hear you. Please don't growl at me like that."

"You're not going to try to back out of our agreement?"

"Was it an agreement? I seem to recall your telling me on numerous occasions that I had no choice in the matter!" The perfectly natural tension she was experiencing at the thought of facing Aaron Prescott lent a coldness instead of a teasing note to her words. Then again, she really didn't feel like teasing him that morning, anyway. There were too many other matters on her mind. Her annoyance grew along with her tension.

"You don't have any choice," he grated, stepping in behind her and planting his large hands on her waist. "You're going to do as I say in this matter, honey. It's for the best. When you've cleaned up the Henderson situation and made sure there's relative peace between Brady and his father, then we'll come home and you can yell at me all you like."

"The prospect tantalizes," she drawled laconically, vividly aware of the feel of him as he dragged her lightly back into his warmth.

"You're going to thank me for this when you go out hunting for a new job," he vowed, bending to drop a small kiss behind her ear. "A glowing letter of recommendation from Prescott is going to make a hell of a good impression on your next employer."

Rani said nothing as she considered the irony of the fact that she herself was going to be her next employer. Her lack of response goaded Gage, and he nipped at her earlobe with something other than passion. "Behave yourself today, woman. I want everything neat and tidy when we leave Dallas. Understand? You will resist the urge to tell Prescott what you think of him. You will sweet-talk Mrs. Henderson and you will convince Brady to be pleasant to his father until we're safely out of the picture."

"Sounds like a lot of work," she noted dryly, scrubbing industriously at her face with the washcloth.

"How long do you think it will take you to handle things?" he asked thoughtfully.

"Depends on how easily Mrs. Henderson can be convinced to sign with Prescott Services." She shrugged. "A couple of days, maybe, if I'm lucky."

"Good. The sooner we're finished in Dallas, the better."

With the logical, detail-oriented mind of a successful battlefield commander, Gage orchestrated the remainder of the morning, from making coffee to packing to getting on the jet. Rani never really had time to think, which was probably exactly what he wanted. By the time she stepped off the plane at Dallas–Fort Worth Regional Airport, she felt as if she'd been picked up and carried there.

"Can't we at least go to a hotel first?" she complained briefly as he guided her into a taxi with a firm grip on her arm.

"Later." Leaning forward, he gave the driver succinct instructions and then sat back in the seat beside Rani. "I want Prescott to know you're here and ready to go to work."

"I never would have guessed!"

"Rani, I know you're annoyed with me, but believe me, this is all for the best," he said sharply.

"If you say that one more time, I think I will scream."

"Trust me, honey."

"If you say *that* one more time, I *know* I will scream!" Rani flung herself into the corner of the seat and glared moodily out the window for the duration of the long drive into Dallas. When he eventually walked her into the lobby of the gleaming downtown high rise where Prescott Services had its headquarters, she felt as if she were being delivered under armed escort.

"Miss Cameron!" The beautiful redhead who served as receptionist for Prescott Services opened her green eyes very wide as Gage conducted Rani into the lushly carpeted entrance on the fourteenth floor. "You *are* back! I wasn't expecting you," she added quickly, stumbling over the words. "I mean, Mr. Prescott said you would be here today, but I thought, personally, that you wouldn't come. That is . . ." Her husky voice trailed off helplessly as she glanced uneasily from Rani's set face to the equally grim features of the man beside her. "Mr. Fletcher? I, uh, was the one who took your message earlier this week. Mr. Prescott is expecting both of you, I believe. I'll notify his secretary that you're on your way."

"It's all right, Mary," Rani said, relenting at the awkward and half-accusing expression in the other woman's eyes. "I'm only back for a short time. Just long enough to clean up a few matters. I definitely will not be staying."

The young woman hesitated and then said in a low rush, "We all cheered when you walked out, you know. Prescott was madder than a wet hen, but I think you made your point. He's been treating the other women on the staff with a strictly hands-off approach for the past few weeks. Ask Bev!" Bev Thurston was Prescott's personal secretary. "She says he even made the coffee the other morning when he got into the office first!" The redhead's beautiful eyes gleamed. "Of course it probably won't last long, but the change has been nice."

"I'm afraid it's up to all the women on the staff to enforce the change," Rani sighed. "I'm only sorry I had to come back today and undo some of the good work!"

"The two of you can plot behind the boss's back some other time," Gage interrupted firmly, starting toward the inner sanctum. "Right now we have business to attend to."

He whisked her through the ceiling-high swinging doors and into the offices of the president of Prescott Services. A middle-aged woman, attractive and professional-looking in a dark suit, glanced up from her desk.

"Miss Cameron! You did come back after all! I was so sure you wouldn't give Mr. Prescott the satisfaction of . . . Oh, dear," she amended hastily, taking in the sight of Gage. Instantly the disappointed expression was replaced by the cool efficiency of the professional secretary. "How do you do, Mr. Fletcher? I'm sure Mr. Prescott will be able to see you immediately."

"Thank you," he muttered dryly. "You and the receptionist can chastise Rani later for failing to stand firm under fire. Our first priority is to see Prescott."

"Yes, of course. Please go right in."

"For the record, Miss Thurston," Gage added formally as he walked Rani past the secretary's desk, "it's not Miss Cameron's fault that she had to return to Dallas. I'm the one who forced her back into town."

"I see, Mr. Fletcher."

"Don't bother with any further explanations," Rani hissed angrily. "They don't make it sound any better!"

"Sorry," he growled as he knocked once on the inner door and pushed it open. "I just wanted them to know it wasn't your fault!"

"But it was my fault, Gage," she admonished coolly, stepping ahead of him into the room. Her eyes went to the tall, elegantly attired man with the salt-and-pepper hair who was rising behind the mahogany desk. "Hello, Mr. Prescott. As you can see, your bounty hunter was successful." Behind her she sensed Gage stiffening. "I'm back."

"It's about time, Rani." Aaron Prescott nodded once with a gracious inclination of his head. "You certainly left matters in an uproar, but I should have expected that of you. Thank you, Gage. Your help in this matter is very much appreciated. I have a feeling Rani would not have returned of her own accord." His blue eyes glinted with grim satisfaction. Rani was getting very tired of that particular look in a man's eyes.

"She's here because I didn't leave her much choice," Gage told the older man coldly. "And that makes her my responsibility, Prescott. You will abide by the agreement or she goes back to Albuquerque on the next plane."

"I understand," Aaron conceded politely, his eyes on Rani.

"I want the letter before she takes another step into this room," Gage drawled. Rani heard the subtle menace in him and wondered at it. What letter?

"I had it typed after your phone call yesterday. It's signed and ready." Aaron picked up a two-page letter written on Prescott letterhead and handed it to Gage, who stepped around Rani to take it. She watched him scan it carefully and then fold it neatly into thirds.

"You'll remember everything we agreed to?" Gage shoved the letter into the inside pocket of his jacket and faced Aaron with cold challenge. "If you go back on your word, Prescott, you'll have to deal with me. On a very *personal* basis. I may not have your clout in the business world, but I have more direct methods of stopping you."

"I'll remember everything, Gage," Aaron sighed. "And I don't go back on my word. You know that."

For a moment the two men stood assessing each other, two generals sizing up the opposition, and then Gage nodded once, apparently satisfied. He turned to Rani. His gaze was unreadable, but the fighting stance of his body was not. Gage was prepared for battle from any quarter.

"I'm going to check into the hotel and handle the bags. I'll be back here to pick you up at five. If you need me before then"—he flicked a meaningful glance at Aaron Prescott—"call the hotel and leave a message." He told her where they would be staying and then walked out the door, not giving her a chance to respond. Then again, why should he? Rani asked herself wryly. As far as Gage was concerned, he had gotten her to Dallas, so there was no reason to think she might become obstinate again at that point.

The door swished shut behind him and Rani was left to face her former boss. If she hadn't known better, she might have thought there was a trace of humor behind his unruffled blue gaze.

"Well, Rani," he finally murmured, motioning her to a seat, "you may have ended a fine friendship. Satisfied?"

"What friendship? Yours and mine?" she scoffed, sitting down and crossing her legs calmly.

"No, the one between Gage and myself! Before he agreed to go after you, we got along rather well. We've known each other for some time."

"If you were concerned about maintaining your friendship, you shouldn't have used blackmail to get him to do what you wanted," she shot back icily.

"I beg your pardon?" Aaron said with polite concern.

"Let's get something straight between us, Aaron. I came back for one reason and one reason only. I'm not going to bother trying to salvage the Henderson account for you, much less try to reason with Brady, unless I have your word that you'll release Gage from whatever hold you have over him. Is that very, very clear?" Rani held his eyes steadily, the intensity of her feelings evident in every line of her body. She had chosen a strictly tailored black and white pinstriped suit to wear for her confrontation with Aaron Prescott. On her feet were black pumps, and her hair was as severely knotted as she could manage. Every inch of her radiated cool professionalism.

"I don't think I quite understand," Aaron observed,

leaning casually back in his leather chair. "I was under the impression you returned because I was more or less threatening *you*, not Gage." He waited, appraising his former employee with the vast experience of a lifetime in the business world.

"Your threats about my future career are meaningless," Rani retorted easily. "I have no intention of going back into a similar field, so I won't be needing your assistance in job hunting. I will be going into business for myself, and the work will be totally unrelated to what Prescott Services does." She couldn't deny her own satisfaction in being able at last to make that statement aloud to someone! It was good to be able to let Aaron know she wasn't a complete victim.

He stared at her, eyes faintly narrowed, and Rani wondered what was going on in his astute brain. "Does Gage know about your career plans?"

"Not yet." Not wanting to get involved in that complicated explanation, she kept her response short, but Aaron wasn't so willing to let her escape.

"I see." He got to his feet and walked thoughtfully over to stare out the window. "So he thinks you're here because he convinced you to come back for your own good."

"Something like that."

"But you're really back because you want him to be free of this, uh, hold I have on him," Aaron concluded.

"Brady explained about Gage being under some sort of mysterious obligation to you. I don't want to know anything more about it. I just want your word that you'll release him from it. I won't go back to work until you promise that."

"You have my word." Aaron didn't turn around. "Will you trust it, Rani?"

"You can be ruthless and you have a lot of chauvinistic attitudes that date from another era and you're not above using people to get what you want, but yes, I trust your word. You've never given me cause to doubt it." It was the truth, and Rani breathed a sigh of relief at having achieved Gage's freedom. Her goal was accomplished.

"Do you know, Rani, that a number of women on my staff were disappointed when they learned you would be returning today?" Aaron's voice was tinged with an amused wistfulness.

"I got that impression," she admitted dryly.

"They think you caved in to whatever pressure I applied."

"I did."

"Hardly. You're back because of Gage, not because of me."

"Does it matter, Aaron?" she asked tightly.

"Perhaps not as far as Prescott Services is concerned." He shrugged, swinging around to survey her intently. "And Brady had nothing to do with your return, either, did he?"

"No." She faced him unflinchingly.

"Frankly, I don't know whether or not to be relieved at that information. I would have enjoyed having you in the family, Rani."

She blinked, totally taken aback. "Enjoyed it! You were furious at the idea that Brady might be falling in love with me!"

"It upset me because I know my son's not ready to handle a woman like you," he returned simply. "You would have totally dominated him and, ultimately, the company. If the two of you could have met when he was a little older, more established . . ."

"More able to handle a female?" she drawled mockingly, her eyes flashing.

"Yes." Aaron half smiled. "Then again, he might never have been able to handle you! It would take a man like . . ."

"Like you?" she interrupted with saccharine sweetness.

He moved behind his desk, leaning forward to plant his hands flat on the polished surface. "Damn right! If there weren't thirty years of difference in our ages, I'd have taken on the challenge of you, Rani Cameron." He ignored Rani's gasp of outraged astonishment, continuing to stare at her from across the wide river of those thirty years. "But since fate makes such an attempt out of the question, I'm pleased to have been the means of providing you with the only other man of my acquaintance who could manage the task. You owe me something for introducing you to Gage Fletcher, Rani. I wonder if you'll ever have the courage to admit it."

She was on her feet instantly, her tawny eyes flashing with barely controlled fury. "You haven't changed, have you, Aaron? Making the coffee once in a while in the mornings and keeping your hands off the women who work for you isn't indicative of any great fundamental transformation in your nature, is it? You still see women as either amusing playthings or interesting challenges. Well, I'm warning you, more and more women aren't going to tolerate your kind of subtle day-to-day male chauvinism on the job. If you care at all about the future of the company you plan to leave to your son, you'd damn well better learn to treat everyone on your staff with a full measure of professionalism. Now, if you'll excuse me, I want to get to work. The sooner I'm out of Dallas, the happier I'll be!"

Without pausing for his response, Rani turned on her heel and walked out of the plush office. She swept past the wide-eyed secretary and down the familiar hall that led to her old office. Rounding the corner, she found it empty, waiting for her, and there on the desk was the Henderson file. Drawing a deep, steadying breath, she flung herself into the chair and picked up the folder.

By five o'clock that afternoon, Rani was exhausted. The tension of the morning, added to the incredible quantity of hard work that afternoon, was beginning to take its toll. All she longed for then was a glass of soothing wine, a quiet dinner and her bed. Rising a little stiffly from the swivel chair, she stretched deeply and wondered if Gage had arrived downstairs in the lobby.

She'd been allowed to work undisturbed by Aaron, for which she was extremely grateful. Apparently he had issued instructions that she was to have full and prompt assistance from every member of the staff, however. The data she had needed had been produced with amazing rapidity.

It had taken firm determination to keep from breaking down and answering the unspoken question in everyone's eyes. Several of the women on the staff said she'd accomplished something on their behalf just by walking out of Prescott Services. They could certainly understand, they assured her, why she'd had to come back. But she could sense the quiet hint of accusation.

Damn it! She hadn't walked out for their sakes! She'd done it for her own. And she'd returned for her own reasons, too, not the reasons everyone assumed! However, she was too independent to feel she had to explain the whole mess to each new pair of questioning eyes.

In the morning she would meet with Mrs. Henderson and see if she could salvage the client for Prescott. It wasn't hard to guess where everyone had gone wrong in dealing with the woman. After having talked to the account executives who had tried to take up where Rani had left off, she knew what the problem was. After that conference, she was going to have the promised chat with Brady. She'd made a deal with Aaron and she intended to carry out her end of it.

"Rani!"

She whirled at the sound of Brady's pleased and surprised voice. Thinking of him must have conjured him up from somewhere, and that was unfortunate. After the long, tiring day that she had just put in, Rani would rather have postponed the confrontation.

"Rani, you *did* come back! I knew you'd see reason.

Your career is too important to you to just throw it away on a whim. I realized that all along." He nodded, his handsome face alight with pleasure and, yes, male satisfaction as he stepped into the room.

Rani glared at him, convinced that if one more man with that particular look on his face walked through her door, she would no longer be responsible for her actions. "Brady, I'm only here to clean up the Henderson account and to . . . to talk to you. But if you don't mind, could we have the discussion tomorrow? I'm very tired this evening and I'd like to leave."

"Of course," he murmured, coming closer. "I'll take you out to dinner tonight. How does that sound? I owe you an apology for the way I behaved the other day in your apartment. You were absolutely right, you know. A man has to stand on his own two feet. I had no right using you as an excuse to rebel against Dad. I realized that as soon as I'd had a chance to cool down. But it looks as though you've had a chance to do some thinking, too, haven't you? Otherwise you wouldn't be here."

"If you'll excuse me, Brady," she began firmly, not wanting to get mired down in a discussion with him, "I really do have to run. Tomorrow we can talk. I'll be very interested to hear what your plans are now that you're back at Prescott Services. . . ." She stepped neatly around him, moving to collect the jacket of her suit and her purse. "To tell you the truth, I'm exhausted right at the moment."

"That's no problem, Rani. I'll take you someplace relaxed and quiet," Brady countered urgently. "Come on, let's get out of here. I don't blame you for wanting to put some distance between yourself and this office tonight!"

He took her arm before Rani realized his intention, guiding her toward the door. She turned a startled face up to him, prepared to ask him to release her, but a

familiar rough male voice from the doorway halted her
words before she could get them past her lips.

"The only distance you need be concerned about,
Brady, is the distance between yourself and Rani. I want
to see a lot of it. Immediately. Take your hand off her or
I'll break each and every one of your fingers."

9

~~~~~~~~~~~

"Gage!" Rani blinked in startled fascination at the grim-faced man confronting her. She was vaguely aware of Brady's hand falling rapidly away from her arm, and then she heard the younger man racing into an explanation.

"Hey, it's okay, Gage," he soothed quickly. "I haven't forgotten what you told me the other day. I know she's private property. All I wanted to do was have dinner with her and tell her about my plans for Prescott Services. Honest!" Brady tried a lopsided, placating grin, raising both palms to show they were clear of Rani. "I didn't know you were around."

"As far as you're concerned, I'm *always* around Rani. Treat her as if you always see me standing at her side and you'll be safe!" Gage glided across the room to take Rani's arm, ignoring the way she stiffened and glared at him. His attention was still on the other man. "Don't look so confused, Brady," he advised laconically as he whisked his captive out the door. "You'll understand when you find the right woman."

Brady's rueful face disappeared as Rani was hustled down the hall to the elevator. "For heaven's sake, Gage! That was uncalled for and more than a little annoying. Brady is a friend of mine and he had a perfect right to talk to me about what's going on here at Prescott Services. After all, he was involved in this mess, too!"

"He's not involved with *you*. Not anymore." Gage's mouth was tight, and Rani could feel the restlessness in his body. He'd been angry at finding Brady with her and hadn't had a chance to dissipate that anger in the primitive fashion his jealousy would have preferred.

Jealousy? Yes, Gage was jealous. Was that so surprising? Rani asked herself. She'd known all along that he was a possessive man. If she intended to go through with their "arrangement," as he called it, she had better be prepared for that possessiveness of his. Still, for the sake of form, she had to make some protest.

"Brady and I were never involved, not the way you mean, but even if we had been, that wouldn't give you the right to make a scene like that. Behave yourself, Gage Fletcher. I've had a hard day and I don't feel like tolerating the whims and moods of a jealous man tonight!"

She was stepping through the elevator doors as she finished that last sentence, and the next words out of her mouth consisted of a startled exclamation. "What in the . . . ? Gage!" He had stormed through the door behind her, catching her by the shoulder and pinning her abruptly to the wall. Rani had a brief moment in which to be grateful that the elevator was empty, and then, almost immediately, she was wishing there had been other passengers. Lips parted and eyes widening in astonishment, she stared up at him.

"I'm afraid you're going to have to learn to tolerate my little whims and moods," he rasped with barely leashed menace. "That's the way I'm made, damn it! I won't have you flirting or leading on other men, no matter how innocent you think the situation is."

"I was hardly flirting!" she snapped back, appalled at the accusation.

"I don't care what you call it. You will steer clear of other men, especially the Prescott men. You're going to finish what needs to be done here in Dallas and then we're going home, and neither of them is going to come near you again."

"That happens to suit me just fine, remember? I wouldn't be near them now if it weren't for you!" The hasty words were uttered before she could think, and almost at once Rani regretted them. Gage's rugged features grew even more severe, if such a thing were possible, and his eyes were clouded with a smoke that warned of fire.

"I'm fully aware of my role in all this," he said, fingers digging into the tender skin of her shoulders. "And I'm also aware of my responsibility. Don't make this any harder on either of us than it already is, Rani. My little whims and moods, as you call them, aren't going to improve, so you might as well get used to humoring them!"

He released her as the elevator doors opened on to the lobby. Taking her arm in a grip of steel, he guided her out into the street to a waiting taxi. As he helped her into the vehicle and climbed in beside her, he rattled off the name of their hotel, a new, gleaming tower on the city skyline.

"Your taxi fares lately must be enormous," Rani muttered, unconsciously rubbing her arm where his fingers had been holding her.

"I'll bill them to Prescott." Gage flung himself back into the seat and eyed her narrowly. "Damn, but I'll be glad when this is over. How did it go today, Rani?"

She shrugged, not looking at him. "As well as can be expected."

His mouth twisted wryly. "Are the other women still making you feel like a traitor?"

"I didn't quit because of them and I didn't come back because of them," she replied distantly.

"But you can't help wishing you hadn't let them down by returning, can you?" Gage sucked in his breath. "I'm sorry about that, Rani."

"Everyone has to fight his or her own battles," she murmured. "I'll handle mine and the others will have to handle theirs."

For a moment she thought he was struggling to find something sympathetic and encouraging to say, but in the end Gage gave up the attempt and subsided into silence until they reached the hotel. It was as if nothing he could say would alleviate the situation, and he knew it. She sensed his frustration as clearly as if he had vented it aloud.

When he ushered her into the modern, elegantly decorated room on the tenth floor of the hotel, Rani walked over to the bed, kicked off her high-heeled pumps and sat down with a sigh. "Where's your room?" she felt goaded into asking, knowing already what the answer would be.

"Don't be ridiculous," he growled, shutting the door and leaning back against it with his arms folded across his chest. "Did you think I would be sleeping down the hall?"

"To tell you the truth," she drawled, slipping off her suit jacket. "I hadn't really given it any thought one way or the other. I've, uh, been rather occupied this afternoon."

Gage straightened away from the door, his expression softening fractionally. "What you need is a drink and a good meal. Put on that thing with the flowers I unpacked for you and we'll go downstairs to the lounge." Not waiting for her response, he headed for the huge tiled bath, tugging at the tie he was wearing.

When the door closed behind him, Rani rose with a groan and glanced into the closet. He *had* unpacked for her. The small gesture elicited a smile. Poor Gage, he must be in a real turmoil—torn between guilt at having forced her back to Dallas and his own personal belief that it was the right thing for her to do. The fact that bringing her back had also satisfied his obligation to Prescott was undoubtedly feeding his sense of guilt. When this was all over, Rani told herself resolutely, they were going to have a long talk. She didn't want him feeling guilty. Somehow she would have to let him know she'd returned for her own reasons, not his.

That "thing with the flowers" was a square-necked dress with a background of dark blue. The skirt was splashed with multi-hued flowers, and the wide cummerbund belt defined Rani's waist to perfection. The sleeves were almost frivolously bouffant, ending at her elbow. The full hem floated around her knees. As with most of her other clothes, the dress had a western air to it, and it suited her when she wore her hair in a simple twist and let the escaping tendrils feather her exposed neck and shoulders.

By the time Gage emerged from the shower, dressed in a dazzlingly white shirt and a pair of dark slacks that clung to his lean body, Rani was dressed and waiting obediently.

"That's better," he murmured, allowing himself a small, placating smile as his eyes roved appreciatively over her. "Hungry?"

"A little." Rani absorbed the impact of him as he knotted his tie in front of the mirror, liking the way his dark hair gleamed from the shower and the manner in which his shirt fit across his broad shoulders. The masculine power in him tugged at her senses, pushing aside her tension. In that moment it came to Rani that she could never imagine herself with any other man.

Before she could ponder the full implications of that

realization, Gage was turning away from the mirror, catching up the dark suede jacket he planned to wear and urging her toward the door. "Let's go, honey. I need that drink as badly as you do!"

The lounge was all dark leather and soft lighting, filled for the most part with a wealthy business crowd and a few tourists who were visiting Dallas. In the pleasantly intimate setting, Rani leaned back into the depths of the booth and gave an unconscious sigh of slowly relaxing tension. Gage watched her, eyes softening as she let herself unwind after the difficult day.

"How much longer, Rani?" he asked bluntly, sipping the whiskey he had ordered for himself. "When can we go home?"

"You're very anxious to get away. We only just arrived!"

"You know damn good and well I want this visit to Dallas to be as short as possible. And I think you want the same."

"It all depends on how annoyed Mrs. Henderson is," she told him simply.

"What went wrong with that account after you left?" The question hinted at a perceptiveness she hadn't credited him with until now. "Who blew it?"

"I gather the poor woman has been through two or three of my successors—all male. And that, I'm afraid, was the mistake. They made the fatal error of treating her like a delicate, grandmotherly type who wouldn't want to be bothered with a lot of technical business details and probably wouldn't understand them anyway!"

"Don't tell me," Gage said, wincing, "am I about to be treated to another example of blundering male chauvinism?"

"Afraid so," she retorted calmly. "What my successors and Aaron Prescott appear to have overlooked in their dealings with Mrs. Henderson is that she single-handedly salvaged the gourmet grocery business her husband left her when he died. It was on the point of bankruptcy and she's brought it back to thriving growth. Fools!" Rani paused a moment to reflect on the stupidity of the male account executives who had taken her place. "They see her only as a middle-aged woman who raised three kids and pampered her husband. What they don't seem to be able to detect is that she's intelligent and has natural business instincts that rival Aaron Prescott's! Probably surpass them, in fact."

"So they've been handling her all wrong and she's growing annoyed?"

"With good reason!"

"Has Prescott himself tried to deal with her?"

"No. He's been guiding his men, though, thinking he knows best how to deal with a grandmotherly widow type. If I hadn't returned, he probably would have stepped in and tried to salvage the account himself. And he probably would have lost it, too."

"Maybe that's why he didn't try," Gage noted. "It would have been personally embarrassing for him to take over where his men had failed and then fail, too!"

"Yes." Rani's mouth tilted upward in her first real smile of the day. "Wouldn't that have been fun to watch?"

"I think," Gage said politely, "that there's a definite streak of sadism buried in you."

"Mmm."

He sat back, watching her with a shuttered gaze. "Am I going to be made to pay for what I've done to you today?"

"Don't you think you ought to make amends?" she managed flippantly.

"I think," he said slowly, emphatically, "that I did the best thing for everyone under the circumstances. Sometimes there just aren't any perfect solutions to a problem."

"And hence war?" Rani sipped at her drink, meeting his steady look with sudden understanding.

"Exactly. Always an imperfect solution but sometimes the only one remaining."

"Since traditionally it's usually men who engage in warfare, we must then draw the conclusion that it is their imperfect thinking processes that make them unable to come up with better alternatives to problems. They seem to prefer to fight their way out of a problem rather than solve it intelligently. No wonder they have so much trouble understanding women!"

He grinned, a flash of piratical white teeth appearing momentarily. "If you're trying to argue that women are somehow more rational and inclined to act more intelligently in emotional situations, you're wading into deep water, lady. I can find a counter argument to every one you try. You yourself are living proof that the female of the species isn't any more apt to act reasonably than the male. You're the one who stormed out of a high-paying job for a lot of essentially petty reasons, and you're the one who had too much pride to go back even though not doing so was bound to affect your whole future. You're the one who does such a damn good job of acting on impulse and who scorns the reasonable, disciplined approach."

And I'm the one who came back to Dallas, even though I swore I wouldn't, for the sake of a man, Rani concluded silently, her tawny eyes turning into unreadable pools as she faced Gage. *For the sake of a man I don't want to live without.* Gage had a stronger point than he'd guessed. She hadn't exactly acted reasonably or intelligently. Nor did she regret her impulsiveness.

They lingered over dinner, relaxing further as they enjoyed the herbed vichyssoise, the grapefruit and walnut salad and an excellent deviled-crab-and-prawn dish. The fine white burgundy Gage selected to accompany the meal had proven a perfect accompaniment to the food, and the combination of all ingredients began to have more than a relaxing effect on Rani. She began to feel downright drowsy. It had been a long, hard day, and there was another one coming on the morrow.

"I know that was a yawn you were attempting to hide a moment ago," Gage murmured as they rose at last from the dining table and made their way out of the restaurant, "but there's one more thing I'd like to do before we go back to the room and you pass out on me."

"Nothing energetic, I hope," she tossed back dryly. She really was exhausted.

"Just one dance." He guided her purposefully toward the lounge, where the warm strains of a dance band could now be heard. "Do you realize I have yet to dance with you?"

"This may not be the most auspicious occasion to try it. I'm half-asleep on my feet," Rani protested in a low murmur as he drew her into his arms on the floor.

"Good," he rumbled into the softness of her hair. "Perhaps in that mood you'll be able to stop thinking of me as the enemy for a while."

She heard the wistfulness in his words and tried to frame a rejoinder. Something to the effect that he didn't have to go on feeling guilty. But somehow it was all too much effort. Opening up that line of conversation was liable to keep her awake all night trying to explain, and Rani was too tired to contemplate a sleepless night.

So she took his advice, encircled his neck with her arms and leaned into the sinewy strength and warmth of his body. Gage's hands moved lingeringly on her back, gliding down to the curve of her waist and pulling her even closer. When she sighed and drowsily closed her eyes, literally giving herself up to his support, he whispered something she didn't quite catch.

But the words didn't matter. She felt unexpectedly secure there in his arms. She had an idea that Gage was making love to her in the lightest and gentlest way right there in the middle of a crowded dance floor, but she couldn't seem to summon a protest. Her tired body and exhausted mind were quite happy to surrender to the wordless promise he seemed to be making. Head resting languidly against his broad shoulder, Rani felt herself drifting.

At some point the music stopped. She was vaguely aware of that fact because Gage was no longer floating her around the floor. When she stirred dreamily and thought about pulling politely out of his arms so that they could walk off the dance floor, Gage's soft, deep chuckle sounded in her ear.

"Go back to sleep, sweetheart. I'll take care of everything."

"I wasn't asleep," she tried to say, about to point out that one could hardly dance while one was asleep. But it was too late. An instant later he had bent smoothly to gather her up into his arms. The next thing she knew he was carrying her off the floor. The shock of being swept off her feet in front of all the people in the lounge permeated her brain.

"Gage! All these people!"

"Forget them. There's only you and me, honey. Go back to sleep."

Lulled by the soothing rasp of his words and the secure warmth of his arms, Rani did exactly that. Afterward she never really remembered the ride up in the elevator, probably because Gage shushed the other curious passengers when he stepped inside. Smiling, they politely held their conversation and let her sleep in peace there in the arms of the large man who cradled her so tenderly.

Nor did she remember the walk down the thickly carpeted hall to her room or the way Gage fumbled a little for the key while retaining his grip on her. She wasn't more than vaguely aware of feeling her clothing removed by strong, careful hands. As soon as her head found the pillow she snuggled instinctively into it, and when the warm, masculine body crawled in beside her and gathered her close, she surrendered completely to a dreamless oblivion.

* * * * *

The bright light of a Texas morning arrived, together with coffee in a silver pot and a dish of croissants and jam.

"Wake up, sleepyhead," Gage commanded firmly, "you have work to do today, remember?"

Rani opened her eyes to find him standing fully dressed beside the bed. He was holding the tray of coffee and croissants. "Are you the bellboy?"

"I'm willing to play bellhop if you're a generous enough tipper," he told her sardonically, his gaze roving across the shape of her body outlined beneath the white sheet.

"You should have taken your tip last night while I was too far gone to protest!" Rani rolled over and struggled to a sitting position, lifting her arms in a huge stretch.

The sheet fell away at once, revealing her naked breasts. Chagrined, she grabbed for it, the heat rising into her cheeks as she shot a sidelong glare at Gage. "Good grief! *Did* you take your tip last night?"

"I did all the work last night," he drawled, setting down the tray and pouring a cup of coffee, "but my only reward was having you pass out very prettily in my arms. And since I prefer you wide awake when I make love to you, no, I didn't get any compensation for my efforts. At least, not the sort of compensation you're implying!" Eyes gleaming, he handed her a dainty china cup full of steaming coffee.

"What other sort is there?" She took the cup and saucer in one hand, holding the sheet in place with the other.

"Believe it or not, I was quite happy just to go to sleep with you cuddled against me," he retorted smoothly, his steady eyes holding her wary ones.

For a long moment she sat there, totally entranced by the expression on his face and the meaning buried in his words, and then the thought of what lay ahead of her that day jolted her back to reality. Hastily she downed the coffee, dropped flaky croissant crumbs in the middle of the wide bed and scrambled for the opposite side, where her lightweight traveling robe waited.

It was while she was showering that Rani's reasoning processes finally began to function again. She did not want the settling of the Henderson account to become a long, drawn-out skirmish. Anxious to clean it up and get herself and Gage out of Dallas, she began to sort through the possibilities.

By the time Gage had taken her in a taxi to the high-rise office building where Prescott Services had its offices, Rani had her battle plan worked out. So intent was she on conducting the opening maneuvers, she wasn't even aware of the anxious, coolly wary look in Gage's eyes as he watched her disappear into the lobby of the building.

One large hand closed into a determined fist as it rested along the back of the seat, and then he settled into the corner of the cab and growled the hotel's name to the driver. There was nothing to be done then except wait. But any commanding officer will freely admit that the hardest part of warfare is the waiting. It feeds the tension, chews at the nerves and erodes self-discipline.

Battlefield decisions, even when right, are often hard. He knew that he was doing the right thing by forcing Rani to take the steps that would protect her from retaliation from Prescott, but Gage swore softly to himself, wishing fervently that there were some way he could have fought the battle in Rani's place.

In her office Rani was concentrating totally on the battle at hand. For her the waiting and planning were nearly over. She picked up the phone and punched out the three-digit code that connected her with Brady's office.

"I need to talk to you right away," she began without preamble when he answered. "I think I've got a way to convince Mrs. Henderson to give Prescott Services a try, and you're the key. Are you interested?"

"Are you kidding?" Brady's eager words exploded in her ear. "Helping you salvage that account would go a long way toward convincing Dad I have a flair for the business. I'll be right down."

He was in her office six minutes later, seated on the opposite side of the desk and frowning intently while Rani went through the facts.

"While you and I were gone, your father's account executives managed to run this deal into the ground, Brady. They treated Mrs. Henderson as if she were an old lady without a brain in her head. It's a wonder she didn't break off the negotiations entirely."

"She probably hung on because Dad dropped hints that you'd be returning eventually," Brady muttered, shaking his head.

"Well, whatever the reason, we've got an appointment with her at ten this morning in her office. I want you to come with me because, in spite of that sad lapse the other day in my apartment"—Rani grinned wryly—"you're still the only man on this staff who has a chance of dealing with her on a businessperson-to-businessperson basis. There aren't any other female account executives on your father's payroll, or else I'd see that the account got turned over to a woman."

Brady cocked one brow. "Now who's sounding chauvinistic?"

Rani found the grace to wince. "You're right, of course. You'll have to forgive me. Lately I've been feeling a little, uh, pressured by the men I've been encountering!"

Brady grinned. "I know. Forget it. Tell me what you know about Mrs. Henderson. I've never met her, just heard Dad talk about how badly he wants that account."

"Mrs. Henderson," Rani began firmly, "could probably run Prescott Services and her gourmet grocery business together with one hand tied behind her back. She also happens to be a very nice person. A rare combination in the business world. The reason I think the two of you might get along is that you, basically, are the same sort of person."

To her astonishment, Brady flushed vividly. "It's a wonder you can say that after what's happened, Rani."

"You forget that I've known you for quite a while now. I know what your father hasn't yet realized: that you're going to do one heck of a good job when you take over the firm and that you'll run the place in a fair and evenhanded manner. I think that when you're in charge, there will be more than one lonely female account executive on your staff, and I think you will also have the sense to refrain from mentioning the lovely color of your employees' eyes in staff meetings!"

Brady groaned. "Don't remind me. I remember that instance very clearly. I thought you were going to walk out then and there the day Dad said those immortal words about having his staff get contact lenses the color of your eyes! The thing is, Rani, that he really didn't mean to offend you." Brady shook his head sadly. "He's part of another era, another time. He genuinely doesn't understand that he's insulting his female employees when he drops all the heavy-handed compliments and veiled sexual innuendos."

"I know," Rani admitted. "And he'll never change. But you're not the same man, and ultimately that's going to be an asset to Prescott Services."

"I assume that you won't be staying on here at Prescott?" Brady watched her with an even, curious look.

"No. I'm going back to Albuquerque as soon as I've placated your father."

"Why did you come back, Rani? Were you really so afraid of him?" There was a perceptiveness in Brady now that made Rani think even more highly of his potential abilities.

"No," she admitted, shuffling papers and spreading them out with a great show of industriousness.

"Rani, in spite of everything, you know we're friends. You can tell me the truth. Why did you come back?"

She glanced up, feeling suddenly too vulnerable. By the time she could scrounge up a suitable answer, it was too late; Brady had already leaped to his own conclusion.

"It was because of Gage, wasn't it?"

"Forget it, Brady. We've got work to do."

10

∞∞∞∞∞∞∞∞

At four-thirty that afternoon Rani stood with Brady in his father's office and summarized the situation succinctly.

"Brady is the only one on your staff right now who can handle the Henderson account. If you want to keep it now that she's signed, you'd better be prepared to give him a free hand in dealing with her. They got along beautifully together today, and you know as well as I do how important a good working relationship is."

Aaron Prescott's narrowed gaze went from Rani's face to that of his son's. "What was the magic trick, Brady?"

"Treating her as if she's one hell of a good businesswoman. Which she is." Brady smiled politely at his father and then at Rani. "I don't think there's any need for me to stick around while you two thrash out your little battle. I've got some work to do, pulling together facts and figures for my new account. If you'll excuse me, I'll be on my way. See you later, Rani, and thanks." He left the room with a sure, purposeful stride that said much for the progress of the evolution he was going through.

Aaron watched his son leave and read the signs. "I may have made a mistake in saying he couldn't handle you, Rani. The boy is starting to surprise me."

"That 'boy' is a man who's going to be running this business one of these days," Rani pointed out dryly.

"That thought has crossed my mind lately," Aaron drawled, leaning back in his chair. "Have a seat, Rani."

"I don't think there's really anything left to discuss, is there?" She made no move to take the chair he indicated. Dressed in a crisply tailored turquoise suit, her hair still tucked into its knot, she was a cool and determined figure standing in the sunlight streaming through the tinted window. Her eyes met his directly. "I've completed my part of the bargain, Aaron."

"So you have. So you have."

Whatever else he might have been about to say was interrupted by a hasty squawk on the intercom.

"Mr. Prescott, Mr. Fletcher's on his way in. I told him you were with someone, but he . . ."

The door to Prescott's inner office was flung open, and Gage was in the room before the secretary's voice could finish the warning. "Thank you, Miss Thurston," Aaron said quietly into the intercom. "It's all right."

Gage's smoky eyes went first to Rani, taking in the tense look on her face in one comprehensive glance. "I just saw Brady on the way out. He said everything was over and done."

"It is," she agreed quietly, suddenly, overwhelmingly aware of the fact that all that lay between them then was the future. The relief and satisfaction in his face signaled that the same thought had come to him.

"Then it's settled, Aaron." Dragging his hungry eyes from Rani, Gage turned on Prescott, walking over to the desk and leaning down to plant his hands flat on the top. "No more threats, no more interference, no more problems, right, Aaron? Because, so help me, God, if you so much as lift a finger to try to hurt Rani in the future, you'll find yourself dealing with me. Is that understood? And I swear I'll take you apart. You *know* I will."

Aaron Prescott considered the very dangerous man in front of him, his mouth tightening for a moment. And then a subtle laughter lit his eyes, although it was not reflected in his composed features. "Threats, Gage? Problems? Interference? Let me tell you something, old pal, I'm the one who's been the victim of threats and intimidation! What's more, I've been outnumbered two to one! I've not only had you breathing fire since the first time you phoned me after meeting Rani, but I've had her to contend with, too! After you left yesterday, she sat there in that chair and warned me that if I didn't guarantee to free you from the 'hold' I have over you, the Henderson account could go to hell as far as she was concerned. Talk about threats! I've been hounded by them. I write letters of recommendation for you, swearing that Rani Cameron is the most brilliant employee I've ever had on my staff, and then I'm forced to listen to lectures from her on how I'm going to run Prescott Services into the ground if I don't start treating my female employees better. You stand there and tell me you'll tear me limb from limb if I ever go near the woman again and she's ready to do the same if I go near you again! I've had it. I feel abused, intimidated and totally badgered. *And if you don't invite me to the wedding, I won't send a present!* Now get out of here, both of you. I've got work to do."

Rani, staring at Gage's face, failed to see the warmth in her ex-boss's eyes. Gage probably failed to see it, too. He was too busy searching his lover's features for the underlying truth. For a moment they stood very still, and then he said rather thickly, "Let's get out of here, Rani. Aaron has work to do. You heard the man."

"Yes. Yes, I heard him." Tearing her gaze from the heat in Gage's eyes, Rani turned toward the door. An instant later Gage had caught hold of her arm and was guiding her through it.

In a fragile, numb silence they rode the elevator down to the lobby, neither looking directly at the other. The trip in the cab back to the hotel was also made in stark silence.

It wasn't until Gage opened the hotel-room door and gently pushed her inside that he finally broke the unnatural, thundering quiet between them.

"What hold?"

"I beg your pardon?" she managed huskily as he stepped away from the closed door and caught her by the shoulders.

"What hold did you think he had over me?" Each word was carefully, almost painfully, enunciated. He snared her glance and waited. She could feel the incredible tension racing through him and knew it was echoed in herself.

"I . . . I never knew what the hold was. I assumed it must have been something rather awkward for you," she whispered shakily. "I don't want to know if you'd rather not tell me, Gage. Believe me. It's not important and it's all over, anyway. Aaron gave me his word that he would release you from it and never bother you again."

"That's why you came back to Dallas with me?" he asked.

Helplessly she nodded. "I couldn't stand the thought of your being under an obligation like that."

"All my logic and the promise of money and my threats of force didn't mean anything?"

"Well, no. You see, Gage, I'm not going to go back into that field. I've found something else I'd much rather do with my life. I'm going to buy The Miniature World from Donna and set myself up in business. There was nothing Aaron could have done to have hurt me in my new career."

"And you knew that all along," he rasped.

"Yes." Rani felt unbearably tense. She hadn't meant

for it all to come out quite like this. She hadn't wanted him to know she was aware of the humiliating hold Aaron Prescott had over him. "At first I didn't tell you because I . . . it was a way of keeping you around for a while," she admitted in a small rush. He might as well know everything since he already knew so much. "I figured that as long as you thought there was a chance of convincing me to go back to Dallas, you'd continue to show an interest in me."

"Oh, my God!"

"And then, when Brady hinted that you were under an obligation to his father, I began to worry about just how big an obligation it was. I didn't like the idea of Aaron having anything to hold over your head. I knew if I told you then about buying The Miniature World, you'd realize the only reason I had for going back to Dallas was for your sake and I thought it might—" Rani broke off and then rushed on, "I thought it might humiliate you if you thought I knew about your being in debt to Prescott."

Gage sucked in his breath, his fingers tightening on her. "This only goes to show, I suppose," he said with a totally false calm, "that every battle holds a few surprises."

"Gage, please, let's not talk about this right now. There will be time in the future, and I meant what I said earlier. I'd really rather not know what your involvement was with Prescott or why he felt he could order you to come after me. . . ."

He gave her a small, impatient shake. "We'll talk about this now. The only hold Aaron Prescott had over me, you little idiot, was in the nature of a favor I owed him. He gave me my first big contract when I went into the business security field here in Dallas a few years ago. Naturally, I was grateful to the man, but that was the end of it! I sure as hell wouldn't go out and do his dirty work for him just because of that! What kind of man do you think I am? He called me up because he knew I was also living in Albuquerque now and that I'd know how to go about finding you. He told me the whole story of how you'd walked out, leaving him in a bind. He was madder than hell, and that's when he let it be known he'd see that you never got another decent job in the field if you didn't come back to Dallas and straighten out the mess you'd left. The fact that Brady had also walked out in a huff no doubt fueled his feelings on the subject. I said I'd look into the matter for him. After all, I did owe the man a favor and he was a business friend. And he made you sound like a rather interesting sort of female."

The last sentence came out in a suspiciously neutral tone, and Rani blinked warily. "He did?"

"Mmmm. Bright, reckless and spirited. He also let it be known you were not the kind of woman who would tame easily to a man's hand." Gage lifted one shoulder fatalistically. "I was curious."

"I see." It was Rani's turn to keep her tone very neutral.

"I doubt it," he retorted dryly. "But *I* saw. As soon as I walked in the door and found you bent over the Battle of Hastings, I knew I wanted you. I also knew I wanted to protect you from your own recklessness and temper. That meant getting you back to Dallas, because there was no reason to think Prescott wouldn't have done exactly as he'd threatened to do. He was mad enough to take steps to jeopardize your future."

"That letter he gave you yesterday," she questioned cautiously, "it was a letter of recommendation? For me?"

"What did you think it was? Oh, I get it. Some sort of release from the mysterious 'hold' he had over me, right?" Gage's mouth tilted upward at the corners.

"Well, you can't blame me for thinking you were in severe debt to him!" she stormed abruptly. "Every time I accused you of acting like a bounty hunter, you went into a rage."

"How the hell did you expect me to act when you hurled those bounty-hunter accusations? I felt a little like one because I was determined to get you back to Dallas one way or another. Even though I knew I was doing it for your sake, it was still a battle and we were clearly on opposite sides. Then, when I finally got you here and I saw the expressions in the eyes of those other women, I really began to feel guilty. I had to keep reminding myself I was doing the best thing for you."

"I wanted to tell you not to feel guilty," she murmured, lifting a palm to touch the side of his hard face. "But it was all so complicated, and last night I was so tired."

"So you came back for my sake, hmmm?" He pulled her closer, his eyes raking her expression in a fierce search. "You came back to protect me from Prescott?"

"Just as you brought me back to protect me from him," she agreed.

"That man played us for a couple of fools, didn't he? I always knew he could be ruthless in going after what he wanted. Do you really think he deserves to be invited to the wedding?"

Rani went very still beneath his hands. "What wedding?"

"Don't turn stupid on me now, woman. Do you really think there's any other alternative for us?" Gage's thumbs worked small circles on her shoulders.

"Marriage?" She pretended to think about it, refusing to admit that the longing and the need in her was forcing the blood through her veins at a much faster than normal rate. "I thought you had in mind some sort of live-in arrangement."

"Credit Prescott with putting the right label on the subject," Gage growled ruefully. "The man's a product of his era, just as you keep accusing. In his view people in our situation usually get married. But somehow I think you and I might have come to the same conclusion on our own."

She smiled up at him tremulously. "The conventional wisdom is that people get married because they've fallen in love. Aaron, I believe, assumes we're in love."

"Yes. I believe he does."

"What . . ." Rani paused to lick suddenly dry lips. "What do you believe, Gage?"

"I've had a few nasty thoughts about Aaron Prescott recently," he stated blandly, "but I've never thought the man was stupid."

"No. Neither have I."

"I also believe," Gage went on steadily, "chauvinist that I am, that there are times when a man has to take a few risks. There are also times when he doesn't have much option. I love you, Rani Cameron. I think I've probably loved you from the start. I sure as hell knew from the beginning that I was going to find some way of having you living under my roof as soon as possible. I need you, I want you and, damn it, there isn't any other word for what I feel: I love you!"

"Oh, Gage!" She was nestling deep into his arms, clinging to him. "I love you, too. I told myself you were all wrong for me—not the kind of man I needed at all—but I couldn't resist you. Somewhere along the line I began to realize that our battles didn't really frighten me. I understood your passions because they were like my own. I've never met a man whose passions were so like my own," she concluded in soft wonder.

"Sweetheart!" Gage held her fiercely for a long, sweet moment and then he asked unevenly, "Do you think you could get used to my coffee?"

"I'll get used to your coffee if you'll promise to let me have the winning side occasionally when we're reenacting those battle scenes with miniatures!"

"Tired of losing?" he chuckled.

"Ummm." She nodded against his chest. "Although at the moment I feel like a winner."

"So do I," he whispered in a voice that vibrated with the intensity of his emotions. "So do I. And all I want to do right now is love you and have you love me."

His rough palms framed her face, lifting her mouth for his kiss. When his lips came down on hers, Rani felt an

indescribable spectrum of emotion pouring from hi
being into hers. There was gentleness, possessiveness
persuasion and great tenderness. There was love. All sh
could ever ask for or need in a lifetime. Rani gave it bac
with an open heart, her fingers sliding up from hi
shoulders to thread deeply into the sable darkness of hi
hair, and she parted her lips for the hungry invasion of hi
tongue.

Slowly, each movement a caress in itself, they un
dressed each other. Rani felt the trembling in Gage'
fingers as he fumbled with the fastening of her skirt, an
she dusted his neck lightly with a kiss. The evidence of hi
need somehow reflected the fact that where she wa
concerned he was vulnerable. She wanted to soothe an
reassure and make him totally secure in her love, just a
he was doing for her.

"Gage, my darling Gage. I love you so much!"

He groaned in response, catching her mouth onc
more with his own as the last of her clothes fell to th
floor. She fought a tiny battle with each button on hi
shirt, pushing the garment off his shoulders so that sh
could find the inviting warmth of his skin with he
fingertips. When her nails scraped enticingly across hi
flat male nipples, Gage muttered her name on a hoarsel
drawn breath and captured her wrists.

"Finish undressing me, Rani. I want to feel your sof
hands all over me. Touch me, sweetheart. Please touc
me." He guided her hands down to the buckle of his belt,
and Rani obediently began to undo it.

The task took a while because her fingers were shaking
with passion. But when the remainder of his clothing fell
into a pool beside hers on the floor and they stood naked
in each other's arms, she caught her breath and slipped
slowly to her knees.

Down the front of his chest she strung moist little
kisses, her fingertips gliding along his sides to the flat
planes of his hips. Across his firm stomach and along his

muscular thighs she teased and caressed with her lips and her teeth.

His fists closed in her hair, tangling there and urging her to him with mounting desire. When she touched his body with worshipful hands, Gage shuddered and drew her up beside him.

"You drive me wild, my sweet little warrior. When you touch me, all I can think of is getting you onto a bed so that I can feel you beneath me." He suited action to words, scooping her up and settling her gently on the hotel bed. She lifted her arms to pull him down to her, and he lowered himself alongside her with rough urgency.

"Oh, Gage. We should have known from the start. This is so special, so incredible. We should have guessed it was love."

He stroked her body, cherishing her. "We would have eventually. Neither of us is so stubborn that we would have gone on ignoring the feeling indefinitely." He leaned over to tug lightly with his teeth on one nipple, and she arched lovingly in response. When she reacted so uninhibitedly, he rewarded her by treating the other peak equally.

Slowly, wonderingly, they stoked the fires in each other, each anxious to please and be pleased, each wanting the other to be certain of love. Gage tempted and tantalized, drawing excruciatingly exciting patterns along the skin of Rani's stomach until her legs separated of their own accord. When she moaned aloud and sank her nails into his shoulders, he made the patterns even more intimate, arousing her until she could think of nothing else except him.

Rani's hands slid lovingly along his body, clenching deeply into his buttocks and forcing a sharp-edged groan from him. One heavy thigh settled between hers, trapping her deliciously.

"My passionate captive," he drawled sensually. "I shall

never grow tired of carrying you off the battlefield and back to my bed." He stroked the exposed and vulnerable silk of her inner thigh with excitingly rough fingers, and Rani shifted restlessly. Through passionately heavy lashes she studied the craggy features above her.

"Are you sure I'm the prisoner here?" she taunted, touching him with daring intimacy.

The hardness of his body seemed to tighten further under her caress, and he groaned again, seeking the curve of her throat with his lips. "No," Gage admitted raggedly. "I think I'm the one who's being carried off in chains. Take me, sweetheart. Take me and love me!"

She responded to the entreaty with a whispered sigh, flowing over him and onto him. Pushing him down beneath her, she gloried in the voluptuous assault. His hands spanned her waist as she straddled his thighs.

Gingerly, seeking to tease him yet further, she hovered just above him, letting the fullness of his manhood brush demandingly against her. Her mouth curved upward with ancient witchcraft, and she let her fingertips dance across his flesh invitingly.

"Come here and love me, honey," he urged, gently trying to guide her down onto him completely. "I need you so badly."

"In a moment, darling. In a moment."

Something flickered in his eyes, and he must have seen the feminine taunt in her, because the hands at her waist were suddenly no longer gentle and coaxing.

"Now," he instructed thickly. "I need you *now*."

Helpless to resist the strength of his hands, Rani lost the small battle and found herself compelled to accept the thrilling invasion of her body. She called out his name and sprawled across his chest as he gathered her to him. Then his fingers found the full curve of her buttocks, and he held her in place while he began to move against her, into her.

Bound in his embrace, Rani gave herself up to the

surging rhythm, delighting in the sensation of becoming one with the man she loved. She nipped passionately at his shoulder as he drew her into the tightening spiral of ecstasy, and he growled a husky response. Then, as the room seemed to spin around, she found herself being propelled onto her back.

Never breaking the sensual contact between them, Gage followed, whispering incredibly exciting words of love into her ears as he came down on top of her. The raging, primitive skirmish flared into full-fledged war, enmeshing both warriors so deeply that neither could have retreated.

"Gage!" Rani felt the approaching surrender, sensed that he was right behind her, and then it was upon her.

Gage knew the keen satisfaction of having his woman find the ultimate pleasure in his arms, and it fed his own passion. When she shuddered delicately beneath him, her eyes tightly closed in ecstasy, he abandoned himself on the same field of battle.

Rani heard her name torn from his throat and clung more tightly than ever as they swept from war to peace in a heedless, headlong rush of fulfillment.

"My God, Rani. Oh, my God!"

Safe in each other's arms, they lay in a tangle of legs, their bodies flushed and glowing with the sheen of their love. Wordlessly they waded through the foggy aftermath until the mists began to clear and a sense of the present returned.

"I think," Gage announced consideringly, "that I'm starving."

"You're so romantic," Rani said, elevating herself slowly on one elbow to peer at the clock beside the bed. "It's only six. How can you be starving already? Didn't you eat lunch?"

"Nope."

She flicked an astonished look down at him.

"I was too tense to eat," he explained wryly.

"Tense!"

"Yeah, you've really had me on edge lately and you know it! I spent today worrying about everything from Mrs. Henderson's reactions to Brady's. Not to mention Aaron's!"

"Brady's reactions? What are you talking about?" she asked, frowning.

"I had a flash of fear that he might have been one of your reasons for coming back to Dallas. After I found him in your office yesterday afternoon, I began to sweat that one out," Gage confessed.

"Brady and I have never been more than friends, Gage."

"I was sure of that intellectually, but battles aren't always fought on an intellectual level. At any rate, on top of that I was worrying about Aaron."

"Wondering if he'd keep his word about not interfering in my job prospects?"

"Wondering if he would make a pass at you. Offer you an affair or something. The poor man's fascinated by you. He doesn't fully understand you and he'd like to reach out and take you. Don't tell me you didn't realize that," Gage added skeptically as her eyes widened.

Rani remembered the river of thirty years that separated Aaron Prescott from her. The memory of the half-concealed interest in his eyes returned. Instinctively she shook her head once. "He told me himself he was too old for me," she admitted in a whisper.

"Thank God," Gage retorted grimly. "Otherwise I have a feeling he and I would have done more than yell at each other about you. We probably would have gone to war over the matter!"

"No. I could never have loved him, Gage," she said with great certainty. "He would never have understood me in a million years."

"I'm not sure he would have let that stand in his way." Gage grinned, ruffling her hair lovingly. "I don't always understand you, and I sure as hell don't intend to let it stand in *my* way!"

She laughed delightedly. "I've said from the beginning that you're inclined to be arrogant and domineering."

"You'd walk all over a man who wasn't."

"Careful, your male chauvinism is showing again. Not to mention a bad case of overdeveloped machismo."

"Ah, Rani, my sweet love. I have a feeling we're going to have our share of running battles."

"You think so?"

"Definitely. But since I can outrun you, I don't see any major problem."

"Egotist!" She grabbed the pillow and stuffed it down over his head. But she was smiling. The prospect of occasional open warfare with Gage Fletcher didn't alarm her in the least. She knew now how every battle would end between them.

"Wait a second," he pleaded in a muffled voice from underneath the fluffy pillow. "I haven't finished telling you all my worries."

Rani removed the pillow. "You mean you had other worries besides the Prescotts?"

"I told you, I suffered today. It's a wonder all generals don't develop ulcers. In addition to all those other factors, I was feeling guilty about having dragged you back and forced you to face the other women on Prescott's staff. It was obvious they had made you into some sort of local folk heroine."

"I think Brady restored some of my lost status this afternoon," she told him ruefully, remembering what her friend had casually said to the receptionist when they had returned from talking to Mrs. Henderson. "He told Mary that I was leaving again, this time for good. He also pointed out that his father had resorted to force to get me back because it required a woman to get him out of the mess he was in with the Henderson account. Mary liked that slant, I think."

"Good for Brady. Aaron is going to have a surprise on his hands when his son starts coming into his own," Gage acknowledged.

"I think he began to realize that today."

"What with one thing and another, you've had quite an impact on Prescott Services, haven't you?" Gage murmured. His fingers stroked the line of her jaw. "Are you sure you want to go into business for yourself? Think of the fun you could have wreaking havoc among the male-dominated corporations of Albuquerque over the next few years!"

"Is that an offer of a job with your business security firm?" she teased.

"Are you kidding? After seeing what you did to Prescott's operation? Not a chance. I like to run my own business, thanks!"

She laughed. "That's exactly the conclusion I've come to. I want to run my own business. I'm really looking forward to buying The Miniature World. And just think, you'll have free access to miniature soldiers from any era."

"As a dowry, that's irresistible! I accept." He sat up, ignoring the sheet that fell aside in the process, and leaned down to kiss her waiting mouth. "Let's take a shower and go downstairs to the restaurant to celebrate the coming marriage."

"And afterward?" she prompted, her eyes softening with love and laughter.

"Afterward I'll bring you back here and show you some of the finer points of hand-to-hand combat."

"Remember what I said about letting me be on the winning side occasionally!"

"Honey, between the two of us, we can't lose." Gage sealed the promise with a kiss.

YOU'LL BE SWEPT AWAY WITH SILHOUETTE DESIRE

$1.75 each

1 ☐ James
2 ☐ Monet
3 ☐ Clay
4 ☐ Carey

5 ☐ Baker
6 ☐ Mallory
7 ☐ St. Claire

8 ☐ Dee
9 ☐ Simms
10 ☐ Smith

$1.95 each

11 ☐ James	29 ☐ Michelle	47 ☐ Michelle	65 ☐ Allison
12 ☐ Palmer	30 ☐ Lind	48 ☐ Powers	66 ☐ Langtry
13 ☐ Wallace	31 ☐ James	49 ☐ James	67 ☐ James
14 ☐ Valley	32 ☐ Clay	50 ☐ Palmer	68 ☐ Browning
15 ☐ Vernon	33 ☐ Powers	51 ☐ Lind	69 ☐ Carey
16 ☐ Major	34 ☐ Milan	52 ☐ Morgan	70 ☐ Victor
17 ☐ Simms	35 ☐ Major	53 ☐ Joyce	71 ☐ Joyce
18 ☐ Ross	36 ☐ Summers	54 ☐ Fulford	72 ☐ Hart
19 ☐ James	37 ☐ James	55 ☐ James	73 ☐ St. Clair
20 ☐ Allison	38 ☐ Douglass	56 ☐ Douglass	74 ☐ Douglass
21 ☐ Baker	39 ☐ Monet	57 ☐ Michelle	75 ☐ McKenna
22 ☐ Durant	40 ☐ Mallory	58 ☐ Mallory	76 ☐ Michelle
23 ☐ Sunshine	41 ☐ St. Claire	59 ☐ Powers	77 ☐ Lowell
24 ☐ Baxter	42 ☐ Stewart	60 ☐ Dennis	78 ☐ Barber
25 ☐ James	43 ☐ Simms	61 ☐ Simms	79 ☐ Simms
26 ☐ Palmer	44 ☐ West	62 ☐ Monet	80 ☐ Palmer
27 ☐ Conrad	45 ☐ Clay	63 ☐ Dee	81 ☐ Kennedy
28 ☐ Lovan	46 ☐ Chance	64 ☐ Milan	82 ☐ Clay

YOU'LL BE SWEPT AWAY WITH SILHOUETTE DESIRE

$1.95 each

83 ☐ Chance	88 ☐ Trevor	93 ☐ Berk	98 ☐ Joyce
84 ☐ Powers	89 ☐ Ross	94 ☐ Robbins	99 ☐ Major
85 ☐ James	90 ☐ Roszel	95 ☐ Summers	100 ☐ Howard
86 ☐ Malek	91 ☐ Browning	96 ☐ Milan	101 ☐ Morgan
87 ☐ Michelle	92 ☐ Carey	97 ☐ James	102 ☐ Palmer

Get 6 new
Silhouette Special Editions
every month
for a 15–day FREE trial!

Free Home Delivery, Free Previews, Free Bonus Books.
Silhouette Special Editions are a new kind of romance
novel. These are big, powerful stories that will capture
your imagination. They're longer, with fully developed
characters and intricate plots that will hold you spell-
bound from the first page to the very last.

Each month we will send you six exciting *new*
Silhouette Special Editions, just as soon as they are published. If you enjoy them as much as we think you will,
pay the invoice enclosed with your shipment. **They're
delivered right to your door with never a charge for
postage or handling, and there's no obligation to buy
anything at any time.** To start receiving Silhouette Special
Editions regularly, mail the coupon below today.

Silhouette Special Edition

Silhouette Special Editions® **Dept.** SESD 7V
120 Brighton Road, Clifton, NJ 07012

Please send me 6 Silhouette Special Editions, absolutely free,
to look over for 15 days. If not delighted, I will return only 5
and owe nothing.

NAME_____

ADDRESS_____

CITY_____

STATE_____ ZIP_____

SIGNATURE_____

(If under 18, parent or guardian must sign.)

This offer expires July 31, 1984.

Silhouette Special Editions ®is a registered trademark of Simon & Schuster

READERS' COMMENTS ON SILHOUETTE DESIRES

"Thank you for Silhouette Desires. They are the best thing that has happened to the bookshelves in a long time."
—V.W.*, Knoxville, TN

"Silhouette Desires—wonderful, fantastic—the best romance around."
—H.T.*, Margate, N.J.

"As a writer as well as a reader of romantic fiction, I found DESIREs most refreshingly realistic—and definitely as magical as the love captured on their pages."
—C.M.*, Silver Lake, N.Y.

*names available on request

Enjoy love and passion, larger than life!

Let new Silhouette Intimate Moments romance novels take you to the world of your dreams ...and beyond.

Try them for 15 days, free.

Our new series, Silhouette Intimate Moments, is so full of love and excitement, you won't be able to put these books down. We've developed these books for a special kind of reader—one who isn't afraid to be swept away by passion and adventure.

The characters lead thrilling lives—and their feelings are as real and intimate as yours. So you'll share all the joys and sorrows of each heroine.

Enjoy 4 books, free, for 15 days...

When you mail this coupon, we'll send you 4 Silhouette Intimate Moments novels to look over for 15 days. If you're not delighted, simply return them and owe nothing. But if you enjoy them as much as we think you will, just pay the invoice, and we'll send you 4 books each month, as soon as they are published. And there's never a charge for postage or handling!

Mail the coupon below right now. And soon you'll read novels that capture your imagination and carry you away to the world you've always dreamed of!

MAIL TODAY

Silhouette Dept. PCSD11
120 Brighton Road, Box 5020, Clifton, NJ 07015

Yes! I want to be swept away by passion and adventure. Please send me 4 Silhouette Intimate Moments novels each month as soon as they are published. The books are mine to keep for 15 days, free. If not delighted, I can return them and owe nothing. If I decide to keep them, I will pay the enclosed invoice. There's never a charge for convenient home delivery—no postage, handling, or any other hidden charges.

I understand there is no minimum number of books I must buy, and that I can cancel this arrangement at any time.

Name _____

Address _____

City _____ State _____ Zip _____

Signature _____ (If under 18, parent or guardian must sign.)

This offer expires July 31, 1984. Prices and terms subject to change.